MINOR MURDERS

By Joe L. Hensley

MINOR MURDERS
A KILLING IN GOLD
RIVERTOWN RISK
SONG OF CORPUS JURIS
THE POISON SUMMER
LEGISLATIVE BODY
DELIVER US TO EVIL
THE COLOR OF HATE

MINOR MURDERS

JOE L. HENSLEY

PUBLISHED FOR THE CRIME CLUB BY
DOUBLEDAY & COMPANY, INC.
GARDEN CITY, NEW YORK
1979

All of the characters in this book are fictitious, and any resemblance to actual persons, living or dead, is purely coincidental.

Library of Congress Cataloging in Publication Data

Hensley, Joe L   1926–
Minor murders.

I. Title.
PZ4.H525Mi   [PS3558.E55]   813'.5'4

First Edition

ISBN: 0-385-15136-5
Library of Congress Catalog Card Number 78–22735
Copyright © 1979 by Joe L. Hensley
All Rights Reserved
Printed in the United States of America

MINOR
MURDERS

CHAPTER I

Every jail in this state shall provide a special area, separate from the adult area, for juveniles.

I must work and it had not been recently rewarding. Two weeks before I'd jury-lost a damage suit in which the injuries had been substantial, but the liability obscure. Months of work for a verdict of zero. Nothing to show for it except a disgruntled client who had publicly stated "he didn't see how we could have lost." So, when approached, I went to see the girl in juvenile detention who'd been so much in the news, particularly in the Bington *Chronicle,* in recent days.

The juvenile area was in the middle of the rebuilt, "modern" jail, but it still smelled and looked like jail. From around the corner, where adult prisoners awaited trial or served out short time, I could hear one of those adult prisoners cursing. He'd been cursing all the time I'd been in there, pausing only for breath, moderately inventive. There was supposed to be a door between juvenile and adult areas, but it had never been installed, despite the nasty reports of occasional state jail inspectors.

The face of my young, possible client was illuminated from above by the light of a single fifty-watt bulb encased in wire reinforced plastic. Her name was Cheryl "Cherry"

Rettner. I'd seen a letter to the daily newspaper which referred to her as "Cherry the Cutter." She was sixteen years old, soon to be seventeen, about five and a half feet tall, blue-eyed, golden-haired, strongly, even lushly built. She wore tight jeans and a pullover shirt which fought for shapelessness without getting even close. She coolly ignored the curser and smiled now and then at me, apparently intrigued that I'd come to see her.

The probation officer had confided to me that she thought the girl adorable, but that confidence had been terminated by a kind of shudder and a sidewise, curious glance at me, dirty-old-man Robak, messing with the rough element again. Circuit Judge Steinmetz, a friend, had told me gruffly, as we passed in the parking lot, to *watch her*. New Sheriff Abe Dorsett, also a friend, had shaken his head in mock disbelief when I'd requested to be admitted to interview her. Then he'd coyly told me about a thirteen-year-old with a size thirty-six-B bra he'd had in as a temporary guest of his facilities the weekend before. She'd been picked up for "doing it" and charging cash.

Cheryl had a very acute problem. I'd read about it at blood-spattered length in the Bington *Chronicle*. I'd heard about it also on area radio and television. She'd been recently indicted for killing her foster parents with a knife. The media reports made it appear as if her conviction was imminent.

She had a good young smile and she kept using it on me. Probably someone had told her to do that, smile a lot. Our high schools sometimes ignore the frills these days, like reading and writing, but they do have excellent courses in the related fields of personality development and *getting your own way* in this life.

"Your sister Marla sent me over to see you," I explained. "She's asked me to defend you. I told her I'd at least talk with you about it."

"Oh!" she said, seemingly distressed. "She shouldn't have done that. That old bald judge told me he'd appoint someone to defend me. I thought maybe he might have appointed you."

"Would you prefer someone else?" I asked, not that much upset about it.

"No. Oh no, it ain't that. You'd be just great, Mr. Robak. I've heard about you. It's just the money. I hate for Marla to have to spend her money. We're not really that close even if we are sisters. She's almost twice my age."

I'd already figured that. Marla looked to be about thirty at my inspection, a handsome woman, intricately constructed. She was the newest of the girls working at the downtown Moose, the quiet one, the secret smiler, a fantastic figure and a cool face. Those who'd moved in on her had reported quick frustration. She was courteous with drinks and ordered food, but it was as if she existed on two planes, one smiling and helpful, the other reticent and aloof.

"Has anyone been in and asked you questions about what happened?" I asked.

"Uh huh. A couple of men, policemen, came in and asked me some stuff. They told me I didn't have to talk without a lawyer being present and Angler had already told me not to say anything. But I didn't see no real harm and so I went on and talked with them some. One used a tape recorder. I don't know their names, but I've seen them around before. They're juvenile officers I guess. At least one of them is, because he's arrested me before."

"No one was here with you when they asked the questions? I mean like your sister or someone?"

She shook her head firmly. I was a little encouraged. A lot of persons accused of crimes talk themselves into convictions despite Miranda warnings.

"Did you sign anything?"

Again the head shake.

"Tell me exactly what you told them to the best of your recollection."

"I told them the truth and that was pretty much next to nothing. I told them I didn't remember much about what happened. I get these attacks. I've been having them for a long time, since I was small I guess. I get upset, then I get afraid and mad. Things taste funny and smell bad. All of that makes me sicker. I'm supposed to take some stuff for the attacks."

"What kind of attacks?"

"Epilepsy. I've got epilepsy. The medicine ran out and they wouldn't get me any more, can you believe it? I asked lots of times for it." She nodded. "The police kept telling me what had happened and what I did, what Angler and the rest out there said they heard. It was my knife, but they knew that. Things got heavy at school, so I got the knife. I guess I shouldn't have done that, huh?"

"Heavy?"

"People were pushing me. I don't like pushing." She surveyed me with unapologetic blue eyes.

I nodded and thought. If what I'd read and heard was

right then what she'd told the police wouldn't add much to their weaponry. It would be only cumulative, something else to parade in front of a jury during the long, weary trial. The news stories had indicated there were "witnesses," but sometimes (rarely?) newspapers exaggerate. The prosecutor had said he had a good case, but I knew Herman Leaks, the prosecutor, well enough to know he might have difficulty recognizing a good case. I'd have to check. How she got the knife was important. Also, right now, I didn't want her to further complicate her situation by talking with the wrong people, like police officers or the prosecutor.

"Who pushed you?"

She looked away. "Kids. Some kids at school."

"Okay. Where'd you get the knife?"

"I got it from a friend."

"Who?"

"Just a friend. You wouldn't know him." She shook her head. "Or maybe you would."

"Tell me the name. I need to talk with whoever gave it to you. If I can show you got the knife for some foreign purpose it could help you."

She considered it for a moment. "You know Cyclops?" she asked.

"I know him a little. You got it from him, then? From Cyclops?"

She nodded. "Sure. He loaned it to me."

"What did you tell him in order to get him to loan it to you? You must have told him something."

She shrugged. "Just what I'm telling you. That it got heavy at school. That people were bugging me. Cyclops likes me." She giggled. "He's sort of short in the head. I tell him to do something and he does it right away. Anything."

"Does your borrowing the knife from him have anything to it which can come up in the future and hurt your case? You didn't, for example, tell him you were going to use it on anyone, did you? I need to know."

She shook her head violently. "No." She thought for a moment. "I just borrowed it for a while is all."

I wasn't sure she was telling me all the truth. They have a peculiar code at the teen level. You can get through it and crack them open like morning eggs if you hit just the right combination, but you usually only wind up confused otherwise.

"All right," I said, giving up further exploration into the reasons why she'd obtained the knife for now. "What's done's done. From now on I don't want you to say anything to anyone without me being present, no matter how harmless the questions. Can you promise that and stick with it?"

She nodded.

"There'll be one exception. I've got a doctor I want to have examine you. His name's Buckner, Dr. Hugo Buckner." I reached for my billfold and pulled out a dollar and gave it to her. "Give him this. It sort of completes the doctor-patient relationship. Then you can answer his questions. But talk to no one else."

"How about my sister when she comes in to visit me?"

"No, not even her," I cautioned. "Under certain circumstances she might be forced to tell what you'd said. Tell her to talk to me about your case. What you say to me and I then repeat to her isn't admissible and can't hurt you. Just don't talk with anyone about what happened or could have happened the night those people died or before or after it. If I know our local law it's possible they might try putting someone in here close to you to try to get you to talk. So don't let that happen."

She gave me a look. I thought there was a little admiration in it, mixed with some other things I couldn't fathom.

"You're kind of cute for an older guy," she said. She took a soft step closer to the bars of her cage.

"Thank you."

"Get me out of this place and I'll do some things for you."

She must have read the semishocked reaction in my eyes. She stepped back, looked demure, and fell silent for a time so we could both forget it.

"Tell me what you do remember about what happened?" I asked, to start her again.

She said, "The last thing I can remember that really stands out was hearing Mom Davidson across the hall locking up the dorm rooms. That was so the boys couldn't get out. The room I had with Kate they left open usually. I was already feeling kind of bad and I remember that hearing her out there with the locks made me mad and pretty scared. Then I also remember colors and smells, but nothing else, nothing at all."

"You knew you were going to have an attack?" I asked.

"I guess so. Sometimes it will start and then go away, but that's when I use the pills."

"What sort of warning did you get?" I asked, not really knowing about that sort of thing, but seeing an opening in the case against her, wanting to learn.

"I just sort of know. I get nervous. I was nervous all that day, light-headed, jangly like. Funny smells and a bad taste in my mouth. And I was scared. God, how I was scared." A golden curl fell cunningly down on her forehead and she brushed at it with one hand.

I figured in front of a carefully picked jury I could get her out of many things, but not murder. The news had reported Arthur Davidson had died almost instantaneously from two deep and savage stab wounds in his back. Mom Davidson had been mildly mutilated after death. A jury was going to see the pictures of the dead, hear reams of testimony, how they were found, how they were examined, of what they died. That jury would be unused to violence and they'd surely want to punish someone for the two killings. Juries have no equipment and no training to determine relative guilt. They tend to ignore and disbelieve insanity pleas when someone has died. Cheryl Rettner was going to be there before them, described by a host of witnesses, pointed out as the owner or operator of the bloody knife, wearer of the bloody clothes, caught soon after the act, the only show in town.

In my state juveniles are tried as adults for only a few crimes. Murder was the major such crime. Now it was almost summer and I'd be faced with a cornered and harried prosecutor running for his political life against strong opposition. *Election time come fall.* He'd need to look good on this one.

"I wish I could remember more about it," she said, watching me, trying to read my reaction. I thought she was aware of the basic weakness in her story. *How do you kill and not remember?*

"I told those police what I remembered and I'm still in jail." She shook her head. "Maybe remembering more wouldn't help."

"Perhaps." To the best of my recollection I could think of no case where anyone had gotten off because he/she couldn't remember a wrongful, criminal act.

"Did you like the Davidsons?"

"Not me. No one liked the Davidsons." She shook her head. "The paper keeps calling them my foster parents, but all they did was keep me for welfare money." She smiled without humor, almost a grimace. "The Davidsons were nothing to me or anyone else. You ask around, Mr. Robak. You'll find out welfare stopped putting real young kids with them. One young one wound up in a hospital and it made a little smell before it quieted down. A six-year-old boy. They beat him real bad because he wasn't bright enough to be toilet trained too well."

"Did they ever beat you?"

"Not me, Mr. Robak. They knew damned well it wasn't safe. Angler told me sometimes they'd do things to me when I was out of my head."

"What kind of things?"

"Not much. I guess maybe he'd fool around, take off my clothes, sex things. Kate told me once they had Bishop Shooken come in and he prayed over me, trying to exorcise my fits." She shook her head. "They were such repulsive people, them Davidsons, that I don't know what all they did."

"I just want to know what you know."

"Ask the others at the house and they'll tell you. He drank gallons at a time and was usually half stoned. She was heavy into pills—downs, mostly. Kept her fuzzy. When she was deep you had to watch him close. Even Kate had to watch him, little and skinny as she is. He'd come after anything female when his wife wasn't watching, but he couldn't do no real harm anymore. Sometimes, when she was high she'd kind of egg him on, and laugh when nothing happened. I hated them both. Most of the time, though, things weren't real bad, there just wouldn't be enough to eat and the house would be cold."

"Did he chase hard after you?"

She watched me out of eyes that were a hundred years old and estimated the value of her reply. "Sure he did," she finally answered negligently. "I'd let him sniff the edges a little if Angler told me or there was something I needed or wanted."

"Anything like that going on when they were killed?" I asked, restraining my blushes.

She shook her head. "I don't remember."

I waited to see if she would say more.

"If I get convicted what's the most they could do to me?" she asked.

"Do exactly as I say and maybe it won't come to that."

She shivered. "One of the girls they had inside overnight said the story in the newspapers said I could and might get the death penalty, youngest one ever in this county." She watched me, worried. "That ain't right, is it?"

"You could, but I wouldn't worry about that yet," I said slowly. It was a chance. I couldn't see Steinmetz sentencing her to death. He was in the last year of his term and no longer a candidate for office. Under that circumstance he *might* do anything, but I couldn't believe a death penalty for a sixteen-year-old. I tried to remember his face from the short parking-lot talk. *Stern.*

"That stuff I told the policemen won't help them, will it?" she asked, perhaps wanting to broaden her knowledge of the red-eyed law.

"Probably not. You didn't have a lawyer then. Your sister wasn't present." If they could get it in they'd get it in. Another item of proof. I doubted they could get it in if I raised an objection. I'd not try to raise that objection until trial, make my motion to suppress when the evidence was offered. That way, if Steinmetz kept it out, then a jury might just wonder at what sort of underhanded evidence the prosecutor, Herman Leaks, had tried to sneak in and the court disallowed.

"What year of school are you in?"

"I'll be a junior in the fall," she said. "That's two years further than my sister Marla got, though she reads lots and that makes her talk educated. I like school some. Others at Davidsons' don't. Angler don't much like it. We all get made to go. Angler either goes to school or has to go back to the correctional home in the capital. Angler ought to have to go to school anyway. He's smarter than any teacher out there—tests genius. And he could be a top-rate jock if he'd only try."

"Who's Angler?" I asked. She'd used his name again and again in our discussion.

"You'll meet him," she said guardedly. "He's a boy at the home. He kind of is and isn't my boy friend." She nodded. "I guess maybe isn't for a while. You should talk to him." Her eyes were earnest.

"All right. Were your grades okay?"

"Most times. Some of them were pretty good."

A silence grew between us. Maybe she was daydreaming about her junior year coming up. Except for a few answers, she seemed normal enough to me. Maybe I could take her out of jeans and put her in a loose dress, no make-up, have her carry a Bible into court and keep her eyes down at all times. I knew a lawyer who'd done something like that once with a lady accused of poisoning. She'd gotten off. I kept imagining what probably would happen to Cheryl if things proceeded normally. She'd be convicted of murder. In my state now, juries don't decide what will happen to a person convicted of murder. Juries decide only guilt or innocence. A few years back the legislature, in its dubious biennial wisdom, moved punishment decisions to the judiciary. Sentences were decided in separate hearings. Life or death. It was apparently constitutional.

Cheryl Rettner could be sentenced to die. Probably she wouldn't die because there were numerous steps after sentencing and appellate courts had grown sensitive to public repulsion with the death penalty where the defendant had anything at all going. Most people who eventually died these days were black, and/or poor, and/or had death wishes. But if things worked out I could spare her the trauma of the death penalty originally. I could reason with Steinmetz during the sentencing hearing and there was a chance he'd hear me. I was pretty certain, however, that her junior high school year and many years thereafter were going to be spent behind bars, her studies, if any, overseen by watchful, armed guards.

"Tell me all you can remember about that night and about the place you lived," I prompted, wanting to start her again. "Tell me also about the Davidsons and the other kids in the house. Tell me anything you think might have importance."

"Like I told you, the Davidsons were crazy," she began, trying to oblige me, her underlip caught in her concentration between fine, tiny teeth. She reminded me of someone. I tried to remember, but couldn't make the association. Then I did. She didn't look like her, but the bones and the eyes were similar. Judy Garland making sincere conversation with the Wicked Witch of the West, dancing and singing from faded yesterdays, "Over the Rainbow." A bright-haired Judy Garland. I wondered if she knew the resemblance and decided she probably did. How could she fail to know it in these years of the tube?

"They wouldn't buy my medicine. They wouldn't let me leave. Once, when my sister Marla tried to get custody of me, they fought her in court, got Shooken's church into it, and I finally had to stay out there in the home. I didn't care much one way or the other. Life's a bust anyway. And Angler was there, even though he was weird sometimes." She nodded wisely at me, recalling the world she'd lived in out there, the world she understood. "Sometimes the old man would be drunk and she'd be high and days and days would pass when it was tough getting enough food. And they never paid nobody . . ."

She ran down after a long time.

CHAPTER II

A sheriff shall be a conservator of the peace within his county, and execute all process directed to him by legal authority. . . .

Around the corner, as I left, passing the adult cells, the curser-prisoner was going strong. He saw me in the cement and steel corridor and increased both speed and volume, tagging my name into several of his choicest comments.

I nodded. "That's pretty good." Long acquaintance in the inferior courts of the city of Bington allowed me vaguely to recognize him. A drunk who was also a battler.

"I guess if I keep it up," he said in a tractable tone, "they'll turn me loose before Sunday, Robak. Nobody knows for sure what the new sheriff will do, but Sunday's when the churchies come and pray over us." He nodded craftily and went back to it, working up a pretty good sweat.

Downstairs, in his recently inherited dingy office, Sheriff Abe Dorsett sat at his massive desk, legal papers piled high in front of him. He was a husky, somber man somewhere in the never-never zone that exists between fifty and seventy years old. Four years back he'd retired from the state troopers as a detective. He could be different from any sheriff I'd known during my years in Mojeff County. Maybe he would be. He had the training to be a first-class policeman, a rarity in the sheriff's office, where normally only political sagacity was required for survival. He'd beaten out seven other hopefuls in the party caucus after Dutchie Oldenburg had unexpectedly died, then won the primary from a round dozen. Now he was running in the fall for a full term and would surely win. I liked him, even if our politics were different.

"You talk with her?" he asked, knowing I undoubtedly had.

"I did when I could hear over the racket that one guy you've got caged back there makes," I answered.

He smiled gently. "He don't know it yet, but come early Sunday morning I'm sticking his butt in solitary. Right now I'm just letting him wear himself out."

I nodded and he watched me.

"She's a pretty kid, Don, that's sure. Not as pretty as that sister of hers at the Moose. That one's really something special." He smiled, trying for a reaction from me, perhaps realizing who'd hired me. "They's a lot of heat on this one. Newspapers sending people, radio and television." He shook his head ruefully. "The Davidsons belonged to that big cult kind of church in north county, the one where they play the music and all, the one that advertises in the *Chronicle* against dirty books and homos. You know, the one that has revivals like about every night."

I shook my head. Doings like that were beyond me, although I did free work for a few churches, gambling on a final loophole.

"Minister of that bunch keeps hanging around the

courthouse and in here since the killings, asking questions, saying things, and wanting to know about Cherry. I suppose I should get more upset than I am about it, but he talks like he likes me for the election. I hear right now he's featuring law and order, eye for eye, tooth for tooth, in his sermons. Using the Davidsons for his example. Had a extra-big revival advertised special for this week in the *Chronicle*. Real political, but like I said, he's for me, so I'm of course for freedom of religion just now." He looked up at me and smiled. "You know who I mean? Bishop Alvin Shooken? Wears white suits and big white hats. Can't move close to him without him coming on loud about being called and chosen." His voice lowered. "I hear he does some things he oughtn't."

The name meant nothing to me. "Bishop Alvin Shooken?"

"He's something peculiar, Don. Young farmer I know caught him last year praying peculiar with the farmer's wife." He sat, grinning slyly, waiting for me to inquire.

"What's wrong with praying?"

"Well, Donnie, them two didn't have much clothes on when the farmer caught them. The wife said he mesmerized her. Farmer come in here mad, but it must have straightened out, because I didn't hear much about it thereafter." He winked. "I used to think you might get blowed up for that sort of thing, but now I hear around you're maybe going to get married."

"I guess I am if she'll have me," I said, remembering the absent Jo and recent disquieting phone calls. "Tell me more about Bishop Shooken."

"He runs a real close-knit group. He tells them what to do and when and how to do it. He has meetings every night, lots of energy, lots of followers." He nodded tolerantly. One doesn't tamper in an election year, especially with supporters.

"What church made him a bishop?"

"I don't know. Maybe he made hisself one. I remember when he was plain Reverend Shooken, but a year or so back his rank got upped somehow."

I nodded. I supposed it was fair to reward yourself if the world ignored you. Many do.

"How about it?" he asked. "You going to let us talk with Cherry?" he continued, smiling hard, knowing the answer. But it was safe ground and fit for conversation.

"Not right away, Abe. Someone already did, but I'll deal with that when and if they try using it in evidence. I would like one thing—I want to have Doc Buckner come in and check her over."

"Sure. Anytime. You know that. You tell the doc anytime at all."

"Tell me what you know about this place they were keeping her and the people who got killed."

He shrugged. "It's a welfare house. We get lots of kids through here who have to be looked after, maybe watched, locked up at nights. Judge sends some of them out there. The Davidsons had the reputation of running a tight place. There's one other home and then there's lots of foster homes where people take in one or maybe two kids who aren't making it."

"I've heard somewhere the Davidsons weren't very good people to place real young kids with," I said.

He shrugged again, perhaps not knowing, and at least not willing just now to admit such lack of knowledge.

"A house run by welfare," I mused, thinking about it.

"Kids are sort of like property, Don. Until they're eighteen years old, they're really more like property than they are like citizens. I mean they got rights, but it's not rights like you and me."

That was a legally correct statement and so I nodded.

"You were the first one there that night?" I asked.

"Yes. It was kind of peculiar. There was an anonymous phone call. Someone called and said they'd heard screams coming from the house. I took the call. When I got there Cherry was sitting next to the bodies, holding the knife. All the boys and the other girl were locked in. Cherry didn't give me any trouble getting the knife, no matter what the news reported. I just reached and took it. She seemed out of it, very dazed. I couldn't get any answers out of her. There was blood on her dress and hands."

"You checked the other rooms and they were locked?"

"Sure." He nodded. "I checked. Locked from the outside. Key locked. No way to pick them from inside. I had to get the keys off one of the bodies to open the doors."

"How'd everyone act?"

"Nothing out of the ordinary that I remember."

"Where's the house located?"

"Right east of town on the river road. About a quarter of a mile out, on the left side away from the river. Big brick-and-frame. Three stories and you can't miss it. The other kids are still staying there. Welfare got someone else to take over the house and look after things."

"Does welfare own the house?"

"I don't understand the legalities. I deliver kids out there when I get a court order. Welfare operates it somehow, plus others like it." He shook his head. "You positive you want this case?"

"I suppose. Someone's got to do it."

"Okay, but maybe this time it oughtn't to be you. You've had some luck and you've got a little reputation, but this one's dead, cold meat. It could snarl you up. That girl may sound okay, but I think she's got the heart of a tramp. Bishop Shooken's folks won't much like it when they hear about you and your reputation."

"I'm not in business to make them happy."

"Okay, but maybe someday you'll want to get in the political thing again. That group out there's real political. They get down hard on you and it could kill you. You know Wylie Calgor? Run for trustee out there? Him and his wife got divorced and there was a little scandal, not much, mind you, but they beat him bad. Wylie says himself that Shooken and his church did it." He leaned closer and lowered his voice to a conspiratorial whisper. "I mean if you want to consider them a church."

I smiled. "The only thing I plan to run for is the county line."

"Sure now? Positive sure?"

I nodded.

He grinned triumphantly. "Then I'll right now call Gates Taine down at the *Chronicle* office. He wanted to know who took it first off."

I nodded without much interest. I didn't care what he reported to the newspaper. I'd had enough publicity, good and bad, to last my lifetime. Lawyers who do heavy criminal work get it. Besides it was time for me to start some backfires of my own. If I was going to take her case I was going to be her champion. It works that way.

"You giving her medicine, Abe?"

He nodded. "I had the county doctor in. He gave her some pills. I have to make sure she takes them regular."

"Not getting her medicine out there could have been what caused this whole thing, set her off crazy. She's got a brain condition, epilepsy."

He looked me over thoughtfully. At times our first encounters wherein I took on jail clients seemed to be situations where he'd sought my support and I'd sought his. He rummaged in his desk drawer and came out with two pictures which he handed me. The first was of a woman. She lay half nude and bloody on the floor of a drab room. She was stout, approaching middle age. I counted three wounds, two in the side and another in the chest front, right below her breasts. One breast tip had been jaggedly lopped half off. The man was shirtless and balding, older than the woman. The picture had been taken from the rear. He had three wounds also and no visible mutilation.

"She sure killed them enough times and pretty efficient for a girl in a fit," Abe said. He moved in his chair restlessly. His belt and holster squeaked. A deputy watched him nervously from a position near the file cabinets. The deputies were afraid of Abe. No one yet knew exactly what he'd do, who he'd promote and demote, who he'd fire.

"Them Davidsons weren't all that bad, Don. Worked hard out there. He may have drank a little and I suppose they had their problems. But they made them kids go to church. Crazy church, but church."

"Sure," I said, giving up for now. "Did anyone do any tests on them for alcohol or drugs?"

"Not that I heard about. It sure didn't seem necessary. They were dead of apparent causes. Knife wounds."

"Thanks, Abe."

He nodded and smiled again, an agreeable man for now, but deep as a full summer well.

"There could be a value to this for me—having you in it, Don. Find out more for us about that sister of hers who works at the Moose. Even if you get married the information could help your friends." He smirked salaciously. "Now go away. I got lots of business today and there's federals coming from the capital. Someone broke in the farm co-op and stole part of a case of dynamite, some primers, fuse, and caps. Pro job. No prints, no nothing. I need to think hard on that."

I nodded. "Where exactly is that welfare house again?"

He told me.

Outside, Bington blazed with blooms. It was late spring and I could taste the green in things. I looked around as I walked and rejoiced. The dullness of winter and the uncertainties of early spring had fled and now more things seemed to burst into bloom each day. The world had grown young again and I was renewed, if a year older.

Bington was now my town. It was an old town for this part of the world. Its century-and-a-half-old downtown houses, built in the Federal style, were sentinels guarding against the passage of that thief, time. Since I'd come to Bington the houses had not seemingly grown older. A coat of paint now and then was enough to make them young again, but not me.

Tourists came in awe for the flowers and returned in the fall to see the leaves turn. Even I grew flowers in small beds beside my apartment.

Maybe the town seemed young because of the new

crop of kids coming to the university each year, renewing it and so also renewing Bington. But the kids who came seemed to look younger to me with each passing year.

Bington still wasn't the most honest of towns. One party rule had made that ruling party semioblivious to the needs of the citizens, more concerned with bitter, factional fights within the party. The opposition, down lean years, had become tiresome and mostly shrill. But I was comfortable enough and now thought there were many worse towns politically. I had no problems. Once, when local voters had thrown a temporary fit of pique, I'd gone to the legislature as an elected member of the loyal opposition. That had made me into a kind of local legend, the last of my party to hold office. Maybe that record would soon end. I thought our candidate had an outside chance to beat Herman Leaks, their prosecutor.

Recent winters had been long and vicious and I'd sworn during the last one that I'd never complain again about heat, but it was hot outside. I waved at Main Street merchants who watched from their windows and made my way down streets stunned almost empty of movement by the heat. Late spring and the summer that followed weren't the best of times for Bington's merchants. The kids were gone and business was slow.

At the north edge of downtown I came to the office I shared with young Jacob Bornstein. We weren't partners, merely "associated." For a while I thought we would be partners and it was all right with me. But it didn't work out for Jake and I didn't blame him. We liked each other all right. He was enough like his ailing cousin Lou Calberg that it would have been difficult for me not to like him. But Jake viewed some of my practices with alarm and some of my clients with distrust, probably rightfully. So instead of partnership we shared office expenses and looked to each other to mind the store at vacation times.

I'd asked Cheryl's sister to wait for me in the office and then, if I didn't return in a reasonable time, call me the following morning. It had now been at least an hour since I'd told her that, but she was still waiting. She sat stiffly turning the pages of *Time*, which Jake and I buy to amuse and instruct our clients and subtly inform them that we aren't just stick-in-the-mud small-town lawyers.

Her name was Marla Rettner Tilden and she was lovely. Her hair was two shades darker than the blond hair of her sister, her features a little sharper, more distinct. She was about the same height, but built more slightly, not lush, but not spare either. She had a poignant face, sad, lovely, the lips too wide, the eyes too big. When you watched her you could see that she had lived. She'd been twice married, twice divorced. She'd lost the only child of those marriages in an auto wreck when he was four years old. She'd spent time in a nearby state asylum suffering what she called a "nervous breakdown." Now she was an outpatient, on tranquilizers, and a waitress at the downtown Moose Club where I sometimes ate my lunch and many times wiled away my evenings. I'd gotten to know her there and wondered about her because she was, as Sheriff Abe said, a fine, lonely beauty. But I had a friend and so I made no advances.

Today she'd appeared at my office.

"Did they let you in to talk with her?" she asked anxiously, perhaps not really sure I could just walk in and do that even if I was a lawyer.

"Yes. Come on. We'll go back to my office."

She followed behind me. The two secretaries stopped their gossip momentarily and clacked their typers at us as we passed their room, refusing to look up. Looking up could mean extra work. I missed Virginia, once Senator Adam's and my secretary, now retired to Florida.

I sat Marla in my big client chair, which swallowed her. I retreated behind my desk, wishing vaguely that I'd not seen her at the club and she'd gone elsewhere with baby sister's problems. Even if it had been slow and I was frustrated I had things I could do. I didn't need to complicate my life with a tricky sixteen-year-old who was quick with a knife. It was coming on golfing season and, except for an annoying hook, my spring game had been at its best in years. I was making skin quarters off the Jug Hunters, boon golfing-drinking companions.

"They say you're good at this," she said, perhaps reading my mind. "One of the girls at work told me if she ever got into big trouble she'd run for you."

"That was nice of her," I said, sure I knew which girl that was. There was one darling who worked at the club whom I'd seen through the temporary pangs of three divorces.

"They can't keep holding Cherry, can they? I mean if I agreed to take her home and watch her and bring her in for hearings? She's a juvenile." She nodded hesitantly, unsure of her law. "She's only sixteen years old. And she's always been such a sweet girl and a good student. Not a stupid, like me."

"The way she's charged they can continue to hold her. I'd like for you to tell me about any trouble you know of she's been in before."

"Little things." She waved a deprecating hand. "Grass

and boys and running away. Once she got caught in a house with three of those boys out there in the welfare place."

"A dwelling house?"

"Yes. She went into it just fooling around, you know. The boys broke some eggs and scattered things and took a few items. That was last year out at the lake." She looked at me out of greenish-blue eyes, not so certain of my abilities now that I'd failed her first request. "Can't you file something and get her out? I'd promise the judge I'd take good care of her and watch her."

"She's charged with murder, Marla. An underage person who commits that particular crime in this state is tried just like an adult. I doubt the court would even set a bond. If she's convicted she could get the death penalty." I raised a hand and quelled her outburst. "More probably she'd draw a very long sentence."

"Jesus, how can they stick that on someone who's only sixteen years old?"

"It's the way the law is," I said. "They figure a child is a child and should be treated differently until he or she commits a really serious crime."

She nodded gloomily and rubbed her hands together, openly worried now. "Did she do it?"

"I don't know. They apparently have a good case. She probably did it. She was on some epilepsy medicine and she didn't get it. She may have done something during an attack. She acts like she believes she did. I'll look into it some to make sure."

She fell silent.

"How'd the two of you get split up?" I asked. "What was she doing living with those people out there?"

"I tried to get her, but the Davidsons and welfare wouldn't let me have her. Cherry acted silly about it. Sometimes I'd visit her and she'd beg me to take her out of that house. Next day everything would be different and it would be all right out there. I filed anyway and we had a hearing in front of old baldy, the high judge. Lasted all day. I should have hired you, I guess. Davidson brought in some big preacher to testify. He brought a bunch of his people and all of them sat in the courtroom like prim pies. Then there were people from welfare. The welfare lawyer asked me a lot of snotty questions about what I did and when I'd been in the state hospital. I could see that stupid judge looking at me like I was trash to be trampled. He didn't decide it that day, but I knew I wasn't going to win and I didn't. Mom died while I was in the hospital or they'd have never gotten Cherry. Now I guess it's too late."

I nodded. Hearings like she'd described were ordinary happenings in the courts. The simple rule was to do what best benefited the child.

"How about money?" she asked.

"I should tell you that Judge Steinmetz will appoint a lawyer for her if you can't afford one, Marla. You're not responsible for hiring one."

"I want you to do it," she said positively. "I can give you two hundred today and more later, maybe twenty-five a week." She examined me, not sure about it. "They say you're good. I've heard they buy and sell police and lawyers around this town. I've seen people who oughtn't to come into the club and spend too much money—politicians. So I want my attorney for my sister."

"There are plenty of good lawyers in Bington."

"I want you. I believe in you."

"All right," I said reluctantly. I could take a little of her money and fight with Herman Leaks. I'd had pieces of him before and he didn't like me, but he especially didn't like me in court. I was intense and mean in trials and that upset him. Nice lawyers compromised. I'd file for discovery before the trial, depose his witnesses severely, raise nuisance hell. Maybe something would work out—a plea bargain—a chance.

I recognized why I was reluctant. I was an advocate. Once in I'd have to explore it all, search it, do everything I could. Whether a plea bargain worked out or not Steinmetz would be impressed with a vigorous defense. If I created any vestige of doubt in his mind it could affect sentencing. It was nice to believe I could enter casually, because Marla wanted her lawyer to defend her sister, but I realized it wouldn't be casual. It has no worth if it's casual.

I let her pay a secretary, who gave her a receipt. When she'd gone I went back to Jake's office, but it was empty. It was lunchtime so I took the LTD and drove out to a grill near the municipal links. I ate and by two o'clock was with friends on the golf course, cursing my hook, but putting well. I did manage to make one call before teeing off, advising Herman Leaks that I'd be in to see him in the morning. And on the golf course, and afterward, I planned my moves a little.

Later, back in the apartment, I sort of thought Jo might call, so I stayed in, eating a sumptuous frozen pot pie; but the phone never rang. The last time she'd called she'd seemed suddenly tentative, unsure. That had been a while.

In the night I also was unsure. Some demon inside me questioned the whole relationship, making logical arguments until I shushed it with sleep.

CHAPTER III

The term of the office of prosecutor shall begin on the first day of January which next follows the term of office of the present incumbent.

In the morning I ran. I did my customary five miles, medium hard and fast. I've a route I follow. Down from the apartment to the river road. Below that road there's a narrow track that's primarily used by bikers, but good for unimpeded running in the early morning.

I'd found running to be compulsive. It was first a way to lose weight and then a way to keep it off. Soon it became something more, perhaps a way of fighting age. Now I must run every other day or I feel ill and unfinished.

After I ran I showered and shaved and had my usual breakfast of orange juice, freshly squeezed, black coffee, and half an English muffin, without butter.

Then I visited the prosecutor's office.

Herman Leaks and his staff now had their own private offices near the courthouse. A recent county council, rich with federal revenue-sharing funds, had bought all the old houses to the east of the courthouse, put welfare in the largest, public health in another, and the prosecutor in a third.

I went inside and on up to a reception desk occupied by a sour-looking woman. Even though it was early others already waited their turn in the room, mostly mothers seeking child support from errant fathers.

"I'm supposed to see Herman," I told the sour lady.

"You have an appointment?" she inquired suspiciously, assaying my suit.

I nodded. "Tell him it's just Robak."

"Take a seat," she said dubiously.

I sat next to a woman whose divorce I'd secured. She leaned toward me, perhaps thinking to whisper something comforting, but saw the secretary watching and so thought better of it. Maybe I was in trouble. She moved back.

Herman finally came to his door.

"Ah, Robak old man. Come in. Come in."

I got up gratefully and followed him into his paneled office. Leaks was a frustrated man, now forty years-plus old. He'd run hard for the state attorney general's nomination when he'd had two years to go on his prosecutor's term, trying to unseat the incumbent, a man of no great talent. A lot of local lawyers, from both parties, had openly helped embarrass Leaks and beat him soundly because he was a man of minus value. Shortly after his loss, perhaps to show us up, he'd married rich and now he drove Lincoln Marks and smiled coldly at us from inside his closed, air-conditioned windows. He was still mean and useless and untrustworthy. The wife he'd taken had money and that was all—her sole redeeming feature. She fit him. He was the kind of man who was always the hero of every story he told and who never allowed himself to be the butt of his occasional crude jokes. He had few friends. Even the new wife watched him carefully. Politically he was either naïve or dense enough to believe his own flack publicity. The local bar treated him gingerly and dreamed of the day he'd no longer hold office. As prosecutor the bar had to do business with him even if he was like an idiot at a bank teller's window.

"You're looking quite healthy," he said affably. "Still jogging?"

I nodded. I didn't jog, I ran. There's a difference.

"Sit down," he said, smiling at me, perhaps enjoying seeing me in his office, hat in hand.

"So you took on Cherry Rettner as a client," he said, still smiling, this time obscenely. "Has she made you any offers to add to your fee?"

"No," I lied. "Can I expect one?"

He nodded. "Probably. Streetwise little bitch. I got her cold and I'm going to do a job on her. No deals, Robak. It was a grand jury indictment and I can tell you they were one group of horrified citizens. I'm asking for it all."

"You mean the death penalty if she's convicted?" I asked, not particularly surprised.

He nodded, enjoying himself.

I nodded back stolidly. "Okay, but right now I'm working up a civil suit I'm going to file for her, preparing the complaint."

"Civil suit?"

"That's right, Herman. She didn't get her medicine. The county had her out there as its charge and she was supposed to get that medicine and didn't. So I'm going to sue the county. With you going after her the negligence of the county could cost her life. Ought to be worth something." I nodded virtuously.

"You're kidding me," he said, as always not sure of me.

"Not me, Herman. I wouldn't kid you," I said, having just thought it up. "For that possible case I'd like copies of whatever you have in the criminal file, a list of witnesses so I can talk to them, maybe depose them. Your criminal witnesses will be my witnesses in the civil suit."

"File your discovery," he said. I thought he'd been waiting for me to ask for witnesses. "You file discovery and I get your list, too," he added cagily. "It's a two-way street."

"Oh sure, I'll need to do that sometime soon in the criminal case. I was just thinking about the civil situation." I watched him. "You won't get upset, mostly just as a formality, if I join you as a defendant?"

His mean little eyes flickered. Here he was running for his political life in what promised to be a tough year and someone was going to sue him. That was not good and automatically made for bad publicity.

"Why would you need to name me as a party?" he asked, his voice lower, his whole face thawing a bit at mustache level.

I shook my head as if I was confused by it myself. "She was picked up originally on papers prepared by you for the grand jury. I suppose that you weren't to blame, but maybe you'd be a necessary party. I don't know."

He gnawed at the mustache. He hated his job, but he was the type of person who longed for power and didn't exist well without it. From what I'd heard around town there was at least some chance he was going to have to do without power after the upcoming fall election. He'd almost lost his primary and the wounds hadn't healed. Both sides were baying after him. Right now he didn't know whether I was sincere or not. I'd come up with the threatened lawsuit as an inspired move in the game, but I knew he wasn't sure, so I gave him my most solicitous smile.

"I sure wouldn't want to tamper in your election and you know that, Herman. That's the only thing worrying me. I mean maybe, if you were necessary, I could add you later, like late fall?" I winked.

He nodded, accepting my way out of what he saw as a problem. It wasn't one. I could sue him, but it would be laughable. He was immune from civil suit on most things he did in his prosecutor's job and certainly this was an automatic area of immunity, but if he didn't realize it, I wasn't his lawyer.

"I'll have my girl shoot you copies of what we have in the file," he said, capitulating. "I didn't mean to sound hard to do business with, Don. It's only that this is such a tough job, old man." Another of his many faults was that you could fold him like a busted poker hand, in court or out. He buzzed someone out in the far reaches of his office and gave terse instructions.

"You said she was streetwise, Herman. Tell me what you meant. I have to be careful about things like that."

He gave me his man-to-man smile, pleased I was worried about appearances. "There's a report in her juvenile file that says she was found nude in bed with three boys out at a house at the lake. Sheriff went out there to investigate a break-in, found them during it." He waved an outraged hand. "Three of them. Think of that. And she looks real hot, too. You've seen her. You know exactly what I mean."

"I may have to get out," I said. "I'll look around. Maybe I won't file a lawsuit at all." I shook my head. "I'll wait for the copies if it's okay."

We nodded together.

If I left he might talk with one of his more fortunately endowed deputies and figure out I was again tampering with his jockstrap and there would go my copies until I filed for discovery. I didn't want to file for discovery until I knew more about the extent of his case. If I didn't file, he couldn't.

So I waited and listened to his predictions about the upcoming election, smiling and nodding now and then, being a good listener, then fleeing as soon as I had my copies.

Outside I skimmed what he had.

The house was out the river road, almost in the country, at the far edge of Bington. It commanded its own low hill on the far side of the road away from the river. It was partly brick and partly frame, three stories high. The second and third floors were frame and were progressively smaller so that the old house faintly resembled a pagoda. It was actually more Victorian than Chinese, medium old, and ramshackle. There was a long front porch along the front of the first floor and another porch at the back. On the third floor a broken window had been covered with a cardboard, political candidate sign: "Re-elect Herman Leaks Prosecutor, Fearless And Fair."

The roof above was piebald, probably from where spring winds in some year had removed the predominantly black shingles and someone had replaced them with a much lighter shade.

One child was in evidence. He or she stared at my LTD from the front porch and then went back to a book.

I parked and walked on up. Behind me the river was wide, with only a narrow grove of trees hiding it. The yard of the home was mostly dandelions and crab grass. The walk was crumbled concrete, having given up most of its body to the recent harsh winters. After I'd climbed the steps to the porch I felt engulfed by the house. It was bigger than I'd thought when I first saw it from the road. I stopped on the porch and looked around and the child examined me curiously.

"You another cop?"

"Not me. I'm a lawyer. I represent Cheryl Rettner." I still wasn't positive, but I thought the child was a girl, maybe a dozen years old, and not pretty.

"I'm Kate James," the girl said, confirming my diagnosis. "How about you fixing it for me to get in to see Cherry? I went down there a couple of times, but they wouldn't let me see her. That new sheriff is one real bastard."

"Maybe I could take you inside with me," I said, plotting it. Putting her in proximity with Cherry might bring me some positive results.

"Super, super," she said. She considered me from her child's world. "Maybe I'll like you. I don't like everyone. What's your name?"

"Don Robak."

She nodded. "I've heard of you."

"How's that?"

She smiled. "We're lawyer buffs around here. Have to be, I guess. I just know your name is all."

"What do you mean by lawyer buffs?"

"We need lawyers now and then. You get to ask in court. Judge never appoints you." She smiled. "We think we know why, but I'm not going to tell you. It would flatter you and you don't need that."

I smiled at her, flattered already. I looked around and walked to the open door. Its screen sagged and was torn in several places, making entrance easy for the voracious late-spring insects.

"Who runs things now?"

"If you mean for welfare then it's the Allens. No one does real much running here. The Allens are churching extra now. Sam's likely back in the kitchen. He does most of the cooking when there's something to cook. Sam's sixteen. Angler and the twins are around somewhere, probably watching us. They're very good at watching and snickering and muscling people. They're all seventeenish." She gave ages as if that information was necessary to identification.

"How many kids staying here?"

"With Cherry in jail I guess there's only us five now." She nodded. "Me in a room, Sam in the small dorm, and the rest in the big dorm. Sometimes there's been as many as twelve. Once, when Angler and Cherry and the twins ran off we were temporarily down to two, just Sam and me." She got up. She was thin and raw-boned and maybe older than I'd first believed. She closed her book with a decisive thump and hid its title from me.

"Come on, Don Robak," she said. "I'll take you in to see Sam."

"How about you, Kate? How old are you?" I asked curiously.

She gave me a wary look, like a fawn caught napping.

"I'm fifteen," she said surprisingly. "I've been a child for a long time." She ran her hands over her flat chest and sourly regarded her boyish hips. "I hope it doesn't last much longer." She smiled again at me, a good smile. "Follow along now and we'll find Sam."

"What do we need to find Sam for?"

"Everyone should talk to Sam," she said, insisting. "He's the only normal one here."

"You seem normal enough."

"Thanks. There are those who'll argue the point with you. Sam's better."

"Then I want to meet him, but first oblige me by taking me for a look at the room where the Davidsons died."

"All right," she said slowly. "The room first and then Sam."

I followed her in and then up steps that were out of plumb, two flights to the third floor.

"What's on the second floor?"

"The Davidsons lived there. Now it's the Allens."

The third-floor hall was narrow and windowless. Its ceiling was a dozen feet or more high. One naked bulb lit it dimly from a wall receptacle. The doors to the various rooms were offset from each other. The first door was open, but the lock was set, a Yale lock on the outer door, set so it would automatically lock the door on closing.

I examined the lock. It was welded or bolted to the outer door. It had no finger turn for the lock, but apparently had to be locked and unlocked by key, like a cell lock in a jail. There was no way to unlock it from within the room.

Kate pulled the door wider. "Careful not to close it or I couldn't get back in."

I peeped in while she watched. There was an old double bunk bed, a cheap chest, and a bureau. There was a small window. One of its panes was covered by the Leaks political sign I'd seen from the road.

"Me'n Cherry's room. Now just mine I guess, at least until the next problem child appears on our doorsteps by judicial decree," Kate said. She pointed at the window. "She broke that out that night. She was wilder than I'd ever seen her. She went banging out of our room and slammed and locked the door on me."

"I see."

She shivered and took my hand in her small one and led me on. The room next up the hall on the same side was apparently the room where the Davidsons had died. The door was open and the lock was a key lock. She pointed in, apparently reluctant to enter.

"It's sort of a spare room. They used it for young kids when they had them here and they used it for a punishment room after welfare cut off the young ones."

"Punishment room?"

"Sure. They'd take someone in here where the others couldn't see, but all of us could hear, even the boys across the hall in the dorms."

"What sort of punishment?"

"Anything their warped minds could imagine." She nodded. "It finally caught up with them."

In the far corner of the dingy room, which I recognized from Sheriff Abe's pictures, it seemed to me that the wood floor was darker in hue, but perhaps that was my imagination.

"The dorm rooms across the hall are always kept locked," Kate explained, tugging me on.

"Were they locked that night?"

"Sure. They were locked about every night. I can't ever remember not seeing them locked."

"If they hadn't been locked and someone came out of one or both of them would you have heard it?"

"I don't know. Maybe. But they were locked."

I examined the two sturdy doors on the other side of the hall. Both were locked when I tried them. The locks were the same type I'd seen on Kate's door, key locks which could be opened only from the hall. I rattled at the doors, but neither had any play and the locks were very solid.

"Angler tried to bust their door open that night, but these doors are solid. He didn't make it even with the twins helping." She shuddered a little. "When the screaming started he said he thought it was Cherry and that they were hurting her. Maybe they were. I heard screaming too, but I couldn't think it was Cherry. I held the door closed, but no one tried to get in until the sheriff got the keys off Mr. Davidson's body and opened up. Everything was quiet then."

"Any windows in these dorm rooms?" I asked.

She nodded. "Small ones. There ain't no place to go from out them. There ain't no ladder or fire escape. Once a fire marshal came out here and raised a lot of pure hell, but no one ever did anything."

I wanted to see in the rooms. "Who has the keys?"

"Allens carry them," she said, smiling. "I'll bet you a thousand dollars they won't give them to you." She shook her head. "No way. The Allens was supposed to be good friends of the Davidsons."

Whether they wanted me to or not there should be a

way for me to get in and examine the dorm rooms. Discovery of some kind? I might even want to wait for trial time and make a motion to view the premises.

"Anything else up here now?" she asked, anxious to get on.

I shook my head, still thinking. "I guess not now."

We went back down the steep steps. Downstairs she led me back through another high-ceilinged hall. It bisected the first floor with rooms opening on either side, each sparsely furnished with worn furniture. At the end of the hall the final door opened to a kitchen. There was an old stove with porcelain gas-tap turners, a refrigerator ancient enough to have a coil on top, and shelves showing assorted pots, pans, and dishes. On a table there was a bright cookbook, well-thumbed. The kitchen was deserted, but from the porch behind I could hear the sound of doleful singing, the tune old, the words indistinguishable. I followed Kate.

If Kate seemed younger than her age then Sam appeared much older than his. He was a light-brown boy, thin, with a bent look to his body. His kinky hair was cut in an afro, but lacked sheen and substance. Five pounds of hair, a hundred and ten pounds for the rest. He was dressed in faded, dirty jeans and an old white dress shirt, several buttons gone from it. He was peeling potatoes into a pan, moving quickly, his hands adept.

"Who you bringing around here?" he asked Kate. "There ain't near enough to feed no extras. Or maybe this is some more law?"

She smiled at him, not angered by his tone. "This is Don Robak, Cherry's lawyer. He won't be staying for a meal. He just came to talk about what happened to the Davidsons."

"Ain't very much to talk about with me. I know next to nothing. You know when I sleep I sleep, Kate. All I heard was Cherry had a bad spell. She screams and passes out when she has one. Sometimes she does more than that, hits out, gets rigid. She can be mean to handle. She cut them Davidsons up." He smiled, not disliking that. "I didn't hear any of it. Hard to believe, but I just didn't hear. Now we got some new folks running this here hall. But Sam still rules the kitchen and anyone messing with Sam might not like what they eat." He said the last as if he was trying to convince himself, assure his place in the scheme of things.

"Where's the heavies?" Kate asked.

"They're here and there," he answered noncommittally. "Pumping iron maybe."

"You say you know nothing about that night?" I asked.

"Not me, man. I get locked in nights, but there's others heard it and know about it. I guess maybe I was having a bad dream that night. I have lots of them. The sounds maybe worked into it. I don't remember waking up at all until that sheriff come pounding on my door. All I heard was the long, loud silence afterwards."

"Did you get along okay with the Davidsons?"

He smiled. "Nope. So I got a motive, I guess. No one could get along with them and no one liked them except that nutty preacher who comes around to pray over us. When we ain't there, he's here. Almost as much now as before. Kids came and went from here and them Davidsons never gave a pretty, green damn. Plenty to drink and nothing to eat was their way. It ain't that much different yet."

"Your room was locked that night?"

"Sure. They kept us all locked in except Cherry and Kate, and them sometimes. Made it easier for them. Davidson liked to fool around and Mom Davidson liked to watch. Besides, I'm real bad. I got to be locked in or I'd go out and break in somewhere and steal enough to get my belly full once." His lonely black eyes mocked me. "You want me to, mister, I can tell lots of things about Cherry's spells."

"What sort of things?"

"They knew about them and wouldn't buy her medicine. I think they liked it that way. She'd have those spells and he'd get his kicks watching her."

"How about this Angler? Wasn't he Cherry's boy friend?"

"I guess. It never seemed to much bother him. Not that part anyway. I think he sometimes put her up to egging at Davidson."

I nodded. If that was young love then the world had changed since last I looked.

Kate touched my hand. "Angler is Angler," she said, as if that explained it all.

She and Sam smiled at each other. I thought they really liked each other. It was nonsexual, a friendship.

CHAPTER IV

A child is a delinquent child if he commits an act which would be a crime if committed by an adult, or leaves home, violates school laws, habitually disobeys, violates curfew. . . .

Three huge youths came up the back steps and entered the porch silently. I was startled. I'd somehow missed seeing them approach, although the yard outside the door was almost bare of trees and bushes.

They came close and stood in line. They smiled friendly smiles at Kate and Sam and watched me. Muscles rippled and I remembered what had been said about lifting weights. They were bulky boys. I disapproved a little. There's a place you reach where you can be too muscled.

"This here's Angler and these two are the twins, Jack and Joe Shallito," Sam explained. He seemed a little afraid of them, something you could feel more than see. I saw him make a tiny motion to Kate and she nodded.

She said, "We'll leave now and you can talk some with them, Mr. Robak."

"All right," I said.

Angler nodded coolly, smiling at them and me and the rest of the world. He was a sunny boy, small-featured, his eyes set close together, very tall and broad and strong. He waited until Kate and Sam were gone.

"What did you want particularly to talk with us about?" he asked politely.

"I'm going to be representing Cheryl," I said. "She said I should talk with you. I got copies of your statements from the prosecutor and looked them over. They seemed a bit fragmentary and I had some questions. My name, like Kate told you, is Donald, Don Robak."

"*Donald,*" one of the twins whispered loudly enough for me to hear, nudging the other twin.

"Something humorous in my first name?" I asked, wanting to take control.

The twins tittered together, watching me boldly.

"I heard about you, man," Angler said. "You're some kind of legal eagle hotshot. Cherry was lucky to draw you." He nodded at me. His tone and words faded the twins' smiles.

"They think everything's funny," Angler confided. "It's a phase." He nodded at me and then winked at them. Each boy wore the summer juvenile uniform—cut-off jeans, tennis shoes, bright shirt.

"We saw your car," Angler said. "We're curious so we wanted to look you over, too. Maybe you're court-appointed? Is that it?" His hair had glints of red in it. The other two had black hair. They were all about the same size. They might have been triplets.

"You know about things like that?" I asked. "Court appointments?"

Angler laughed carefully. The other two waited a moment and then joined in the laughter. He led, they followed.

"I know. I know it all. How do you think we got in this place? I been through lots of court crap. So have Jack and Joe." He leaned negligently against the handy doorframe, very sure of himself. "I practically got a law degree. So do Jack and Joe. We know what they can do and what we can do." He watched me, smile unfaded, his eyes hot and blue.

The twins nodded in unison. So far neither of them had said much. I had a feeling they were intelligent enough to get by on their own, but some unknown accommodation (to me) had made Angler the leader and that was how it was to be.

"We want to help Cherry," Angler said. "Somehow it'll get figured so it comes out okay for her." He nodded at the others and now winked broadly at me. "We mean it. She wasn't right in the head."

"I looked over your statements," I said again. "They were fuzzy enough that I felt I had to talk with you about them. None of you said anything about her having the weapon before or anything about her sickness. Just that you heard screams and she was there and that you saw her with the knife and with blood on her dress after the sheriff unlocked your door." I shook my head.

Angler smiled at me again and the three edged closer. I felt a bead of perspiration form and run down my back and I was surprised by it. I wasn't afraid of him or them, but something inside me reacted to their nearness.

"There's lots of ways to tell things. You, as a lawyer, should know that. If you've talked with Cherry you know she needs bad to get examined by doctors and psychiatrists. Why don't you go and get that arranged and then let us know what them medics say? We need to know that. When we get called to the witness stand you can just bet it's going to come out the best we can make it for sweet Cherry." He leaned very close. "You tell her that for me, tell her so she understands," he ordered.

"Them people was real bad to her," one twin offered. "That old man was always after her. I saw it. We all saw it. She was crazy with fear because of it."

"Did any of you ever see Mr. Davidson doing anything to her when she was in one of her sick spells?" I asked.

"Maybe," Angler answered, smiling again. "Whatever you need, man."

"It doesn't work that way," I said, annoyed.

They grinned among themselves and at me and waited, very certain of themselves. I'd defended people accused of crime before with similar attitudes, people so confident that their stories were as likely as the story the police reported that they were certain of acquittal. But jurors always seem to believe the police where there are two differing factual accounts of a happening.

"What makes you boys think that all you have to do is get in the witness chair, say Cherry was crazy, and a jury will automatically buy it?"

"Why shouldn't they?" Angler asked. "It's the truth."

"I've been a lawyer for a while and I've been in a lot of murder cases. I've yet to see a jury buy an insanity plea. I know it happens, but not often. I think the chances in this case wouldn't be great. So I'd like to know exactly what you saw, if anything, and heard on or around that night. Anything at all, as long as it's true. That way I can plan for the trial. For example, was there anyone, other than the usual people, around the house that night?"

Angler's eyes flickered. "You just go back and read them statements over carefully again."

"I already read them carefully. They're very short. They don't say anything."

"Yeah. That's right. Short and sweet. That's what we know. What we can tell is better for Cherry."

"Why not give me a statement?" I said carefully. "Tell me the rest of it, if there is anything?"

"If it isn't written down it can't hurt Cherry. You tell her that."

"How many jury trials have you been in, Angler?"

"The law's the law."

The perspiration was still running down my back. They were very intent and sure they were right. If I made them angry could they turn against me and talk Cherry right into the death penalty? How much were they involved with her? How much did they care?

"We'll sure help you," the same twin said unctuously, trying to convince me. "But for now it's got to be between us. Cherry needs to know, so you should tell her, but no one else."

I did some figuring. "I'm going to have to depose you," I finally said. "It can't be done your way. I need to know what you're going to say in advance of trial. I have to plan. I know this business. You people don't."

Angler shook his head, now angry with me. "Depositions. We know all about depositions. I wouldn't bother with them if I was you. All there is now is those statements and even you recognized they ain't much. Prosecutor thought they was good enough after we made him sweat for a while to get them. We three went over them real careful before we signed them. You put us on more paper now and you'll hamper what we can do. Right now we can watch the trial and see what happens and play it by ear."

"You ever heard of a separation of witnesses?"

"No one's asked for that yet," he said.

"I do routinely."

"Then we'll plan for it, but don't do something that isn't bright and right for Cherry. And you know you depose hostile witnesses, not friendly ones."

"I can't do things your way," I said. "What you don't realize is that you won't be the only witnesses. With what's in your statements you won't even be important ones. What the sheriff saw is enough to convict her. So I can't do it your way."

"What you mean is it's not supposed to work our way in your safe, legal world," he said sneering a little. "You got your rules, but just remember that they don't mean a damned thing to us." He leaned toward me. "Or maybe it's more than that? Is that it? Maybe you think that we had something to do with the killings?"

"I didn't say that," I said.

"You don't have to say it. I think maybe you think it. And it's not smart to think it, Mr. Robak."

Something about him made me slow a little. "You've got a hate for the law, haven't you, Angler?"

"I don't have much use for it. The law keeps me from having a driver's license, it makes me go to school after I shouldn't have to, it keeps me in at nights. All it's ever done for me is hurt me. It let *her* take me and hate me. It put me in jails and foster homes and boys' schools and de-

tention centers. It put me on my own when I was eleven—
after she died."

"Who died?" I asked, catching a change in his voice.

He gave me an angry look. "My m-m-mother. She ran my dad off. When I got old enough I ran from her." He waved at the twins. "Historically it was pretty much the same for them. No one wanted two big ones. Now we three got each other. We run it around here to suit us, not you or that dumb prosecutor or some judge. I'm telling you we're on Cherry's side after we're on our side. Maybe you can change that if you try hard doing it your way, Mr. Robak."

"I'll think about what you're telling me," I said. "But I'll still most probably depose you."

He reached out a huge, exasperated hand. I stepped away.

"Don't," I warned.

"I could break you in two," he boasted. "Any one of us could. Just remember you're mortal, Robak."

Some of the heavy muscle builders slow themselves badly. I didn't know about these three. But I wanted no juvenile trouble. I had nothing to gain.

I was saved by noises coming from the front of the house. Angler subsided, cocking his head, listening, a curious, intent look on his face.

"I think our new zoo attendants are back," he said to the twins. He nodded coolly at me. "You go on, counselor. Out the back is best. Remember what I've said. Remember it well."

I waited and instead followed behind them down the hall. They ignored that and moved out the tattered screen door. I stayed back in the shadows momentarily and watched. Three older people, two men and a woman, stood staring at my car and listening to Angler and the twins.

"You say he's a lawyer claiming to represent Cheryl?" I heard one of the men ask.

Angler nodded. His whole outward demeanor had changed. From menacing he'd gone to respectful.

"He's asking a lot of questions and being kind of threatening." He looked back at the door, knowing I was standing inside. I moved on out.

One of the men was massive and middle-aged. He wore a white suit and a large western-style white hat. I recognized him from the description the sheriff had given me. Bishop Shooken. He looked questioningly at the other two adults and I saw them nod permission at him.

"Here now, sir," he said harshly to me. "The police and the prosecutor told us not to let people come around here bothering these kids. It's been upsetting enough on them already. I'll have to ask you to leave and not come back."

"That isn't very Christian, Bishop." Something about him grated on me badly.

He moved a little closer, examining me with red, narrowed eyes. There was a look and a vague smell to him and I thought I recognized it. A heavy drinker.

"Do I know you?" he asked.

"Robak, Bishop. I've seen you here and there in some of Bington's better watering holes." I hadn't, but figured he wouldn't know.

"I do the Lord's work in taverns," he said piously. "That's where I was and what I was doing with my life when the call came to me. I've always remembered."

"What kind of call was that?"

He gave me a look of intense dislike. "To preach, sir. To save those who have lost their way. To carry the word to sinners like you." He paused, watching me for reaction. "Why are you here?"

"I'm going to represent Cheryl Rettner."

His face darkened. "She's the spawn of the devil himself. Punishment will come to you both here and in the next world if you use any of your slick, shyster tricks." He put his right hand on his forehead, meditating. "I'm getting the message now. I know it and proclaim it. She's to be punished."

I smiled. "If that's the way of it I suppose I'll have to talk with you before I take any future case?"

"Don't be cynical. She's guilty. I know it."

"I'd rather count on twelve jurymen."

"You'd be surprised at what I can and will do about that when the case comes to trial."

I nodded carefully at him. "Now that you've threatened that I'll try my best to guard against it. If I see your hand tampering in any of the proceedings, Bishop, you can be assured that all else will stop until you're out of it and until you've been suitably punished."

He gave me a venomous look. He was a man unaccustomed to having his pronouncements argued with.

"Mr. and Mrs. Allen would like you to leave and not return."

Behind him his faded, American Gothic companions, old, with white hair and work-hardened hands, nodded. They had a shared, complacent look about them, as if they'd never made a complaint, always ridden along easily. I nodded at them.

"I'll leave if they want, but I'll be back. Next time it will be officially, with a court order."

"Mr. Leaks, the public prosecutor, may have something to say about that," Bishop Shooken said.

"The only thing he'll tell you is that I have the right," I said, smiling at him.

"We'll see," he said darkly, not so sure now.

I nodded to the three boys, who'd watched the argument with concealed glee. I walked on out to the LTD and drove out.

Down the lane and back on the main road I passed a grove of concealing trees and Kate came loping from behind one of them, waving frantically. I pulled to the side of the road and opened the door for her and she clambered quickly in, awkward and plain, obviously not trusting me much, sitting as far away in the car seat as she could.

"They can't see us out here from the house," she said, reassuring herself. "They'll be looking for me for prayers soon and they'll want to quiz me about what you asked and what you wanted when you first came."

"They were all on the porch when I left. Except Sam."

She nodded. "We didn't set any time for me to come in and you take me with you to see Cherry."

"When can you come in?"

"How about early tomorrow morning? I could bum a ride."

"I'll pick you up if you want."

She shook her head, leery of that and of me. "No, I'll meet you."

"All right. I get there about nine or a little before." I changed directions while I had her in my debt. "Were

Angler and the twins the boys that Cherry ran off with once?"

She nodded.

"How come they ran off? What did they do?"

"I think maybe they ran away for the fun of it, because they were bored. All they did was fool around in a house out at the lake. It wasn't any federal crime or anything. When they heard the sheriff coming then they took off some of their clothes and got into bed. That was when that old gold tooth was sheriff. Cherry said his eyes were popping out."

"Cherry said?"

"Yeah. Angler wouldn't say anything about it when I asked him." She watched me carefully. "He reads lots. Just now he's into books about leaders, Genghis Khan, Hitler, Stalin, Charles Manson."

"That sounds interesting."

"Angler's very interesting as long as you watch him from afar."

"Are you trying to warn me, Kate?"

She shook her head, but I thought she was.

"How long have you known Cherry?"

"Not so long. Since I got put in this house. Since no one would take me. Cherry's taught me lots. I owe her."

"In that time have you ever seen her do anything else violent?"

"I never saw her do anything to hurt anyone, but I've seen her get mad and scream and fight."

"Did she know what she was doing when that happened?"

"I don't think so."

"Why'd she carry the knife?"

"She said once she was carrying it to take care of trouble." She nodded. "Boys were always after her because she's so pretty."

I tried a lame compliment on her. "One day soon I think you'll be very handsome, Kate."

She smiled, not believing me. "I hope so." She opened the car door, suddenly shy. "If you're not at the office I'll just wait."

"Stay and talk another moment."

She snapped the car door shut for her answer and scampered away. I doubted she would ever be anything but an ugly duckling. It wasn't going to be an easy life for her.

I drove back downtown.

CHAPTER V

Expert witnesses, after having been properly qualified, may be called and may present testimony for any party.

The city-owned parking lot near Dr. Hugo Buckner's office was almost vacant. I parked, fed the meter, and walked through the heat across the street and entered his door. I'd called earlier to say I'd be in. A harried nurse did quick bookwork behind a desk. I gave her my name and was rewarded by a slowing of tempo, a long, upward look, which seemed to search me for symptoms.

"The doctor told us to inform him *immediately* when you arrived, Mr. Robak. He *personally* got your chart." She looked me over again. I slumped a little for her. She led the way through the partially filled waiting room, bypassing me in out of turn. She took me down the hall to one of his several examination rooms.

"I'll tell him you're here."

I nodded. She was a handsome girl with a spray of freckles and ginger hair. "Thank you," I muttered despondently.

In a little while he came into the room and gave me a bright, cheery smile.

"I believe your nurse thinks I'm languishing," I said.

"An impressionable child. All I told her was that you were young to be in such a condition." He smiled widely. "And you are that. Your liver could be used to half-sole your running shoes."

"That nurse will spread the word and I won't be able to get downtown credit," I prophesied darkly.

"Credit-schmedit. You've told me many a time that you hate waiting and, as my most interesting patient, I've therefore set up reasonable procedures to aid you. Now you complain." He sighed. "I don't know what to do with you, Robak."

I gave up. In his office, where I was quickly impressed, he usually won.

"I need some help."

He frowned and waited.

"I've a client over in the jail I'd like for you to look over for me. Examine her and say nothing about it afterwards. If anyone asks you anything at all just smile and try to look wise. A girl client."

"It's always a girl with you."

"This one's name is Cheryl Rettner and she's only sixteen years old."

"Then, *for shame*."

"Look her over, examine her, talk with her," I continued, ignoring him. "She's supposed to have some form of epilepsy. She has a history of seizures. Recently she apparently killed both her keepers at a welfare home out in the county in the midst of such a seizure."

He raised an eyebrow.

"Is it possible?"

"Anything's possible. There are different kinds of epilepsy. I've heard of epileptic seizures accompanied by hysteria. Does she claim not to remember anything about what happened?"

"She says she doesn't remember anything much and nothing that helps. It's also possible she may have been attacked sexually at some time while she was in her seizure."

He shrugged. "And she doesn't remember that either?"

"Are you saying it's impossible?"

"Many people have convenient memories. Sometimes the mind will block away a memory, but not very often. Tell me more about the crime."

"The girl had a knife. She cut two people up, inflicting three deep stab wounds on each. One of the people she attacked was a woman. She mutilated the woman a bit. There's been quite a bit about it in the paper and on radio and television. Again, her name's Cheryl Rettner."

I could tell he didn't recognize the name. I knew him well enough to remember that he seldom watched television (except when his beloved Bengals were playing) or read outside his profession. He was the kind of doctor patients dreamed about. He still made time for house calls.

"Okay," he said. "You've got me curious. I'll go over and see her." He looked me over. "You do meet some of the most interesting people, Don."

"When can you make it?"

"Tonight. Maybe tomorrow," he said, slightly irritated at my sudden pushing. "Come back past or call like maybe late tomorrow."

"What are you going to tell Miss Freckles, your nurse, about me now?" I asked at the examination-room door.

"Enough so it could be easy for you," he said, smiling again, planning it. "She's a sympathetic child. I know, with your girl friend still on her trip, that you're frustrated and, shall we politely say, ready. When's Miss Jo due back?"

"Not for a while," I said. The temptation came to lay my troubles on him, but I refrained. Jo Kibble had once been my client and now was my fiancée. I'd given her a ring at Christmas and we'd warily examined the thought of marriage. Both of us were prior matrimonial losers. The western trip had been her idea—see distant relatives—get a fresh outlook. Maybe also wait and see what her friends and confidantes had to report about my actions while she was away.

She'd called regularly at first, once, sometimes twice a week. Lately the calls had thinned out, her return date to Bington had grown nebulous, her attitude become unsure.

"You going to get married?" Doc asked.

"Maybe," I said, not knowing at all.

I own no automatic love for newspapers. The news now gets reported in a sort of competitive hysteria, so that each news outlet, whether radio, television, or newspaper, must make the day's catastrophe seem more appalling than the competition's. Lose the ability to cut and frighten and amaze and the fickle advertisers move on, looking back only to cancel half their lineage.

But my lack of affection is tempered by a recognition of reality. I can't imagine our current world without its newspapers, TV and radio stations, and I doubt that it would be even palatable without them. Also I've found that some of the people who work the news field are the best people I know.

Ed "Gates" Taine was one of them. He had enthusiasm, substantial compassion, and a high appreciation of the ridiculous. We'd kept bumping into each other for so long, over the years, that we became *sort of* friends. He'd been with the Bington *Chronicle* for years.

He was waiting for me when I returned to the office after a succulent Big Mac lunch across from the semisilent summer university. I have an uncomplicated lunchtime appetite.

He stood up when I came into his office.

"I been waiting here quite a while to talk to you," he said accusingly, nodding and grinning to show he was kidding.

"Whatever for, Gates?"

"I'm not only covering the Davidson murders for the paper, I'm also working halvers with some guy who called me from out of town when it happened. He does stuff for one of them detective magazines. He told me he was going to make us money for years hashing and rehashing this one. His New York editors eat up the crap about it being some kind of ritual killing."

"Ritual killing?"

"Yeah. I mean the woman got carved up extra."

I tried to figure something which could benefit my client while he shifted nervously from foot to foot, thin, all bones and energy.

"So you need some quotes from me to feed him? Things he can use? Okay. I protest her innocence. She's only sixteen years old. She has brain problems. She was cruelly and wickedly deprived of her medicine and also constantly mistreated by her jailers out there."

"Jailers?" he asked.

I nodded positively.

He smiled. He knew what I was doing and I knew he'd take it, sort it out, and use what sold newspapers and magazines.

"Off the record, Gates?"

He nodded grudgingly.

"I'm just barely into it. The only thing I know for sure right now is that with her medical condition I may use some novel defense tactics in the trial." I looked at him. "Did you know the deceased couple?"

"Sure. I thought once about doing a story on them and so I visited out there." He shook his head. "I decided not to do the story."

"Why not?"

"I wanted it to be a human-interest kind of thing, but I never could make it work. You know, kindly people taking care of problem children." He rubbed his hands together, trying to explain. "They ran it like a sergeant would run an army barracks, only worse, far worse. I could tell those kids out there detested them." He shook his head. "That old man out there used to be a professional wrestler."

"I didn't know that."

"Well, he was. Course he was a long way past it when he was killed, half made of fat, the other half booze."

"Did they leave any close relatives?"

"No. I went to the funeral. Some cousins came from here and there. There was a will which left what they had to their church."

"Which church was that?"

"I don't know the name, but the one where that Bishop Shooken preaches."

"You know him, Gates?"

"No, not really." He moved back to his original quest. "When the sheriff arrived, according to some reports, Cherry still had the knife. I guess maybe it was a close thing for her. An inexperienced man, say one of the sheriff's deputies, might have shot her. She wouldn't give up the knife so I hear Abe just took it." He shook his head. "Maybe someone else wouldn't have tried."

"And so?"

"It's damning evidence is all. I wondered how you thought you were going to get around it, what you had to say about it? I mean with blood all over her and all."

"Not a thing."

"You'll tell me if anything new happens I can use?"

"Sure," I lied.

Jake sat in his office catching up on the advance sheets. They were paperbound case reports which came out weekly so that you could follow what the appellate courts were doing in advance of the bound volumes.

He looked up, but I couldn't read a thing in his expression.

"How's Lou?" I asked. Lou was Lou Calberg, his relative and my good friend, who'd had a coronary last spring.

"Doing well enough. Rachel said she can bring him home next week." He shook his head. "No visitors at first. And he'll have to take it easy for a while."

"I'd heard that. Tell me when it's okay for me to stop past."

He smiled and I watched him. He'd come into the office with me now about two years back. He'd formed a working relationship quickly with the town of Bington. If there was a fund drive Jake was almost certain to be a part of it; if blood was being collected Jake was good for a pint. He belonged to the Elks, Moose, Jaycees, and the Chamber of Commerce, plus half a dozen Masonic organizations. If he wasn't an officer he chaired a committee. He was conscientious, energetic, and a pretty fair lawyer. My only problem with him was that he hadn't, almost from the beginning, completely approved of me.

I don't always hear correct drums. Jo once complained that if water ran south toward town I'd swim north to see what was up that way. I think what I do is logical and right. Others usually don't. They keep wanting to change me. I tend to resist change.

"I hear you've taken on a new client?" Jake said, making it a question.

"I have that. News travels fast in Bington. I tried to find you earlier so I could tell you."

"No need. I knew it within half an hour of the time you visited the jail. One of the deputies came into Harker's Coffee Shop and announced it rather loudly."

"Well, someone has to defend her."

"I know that, but there's plenty of work to do around here. I need you to be available to help pick me a jury for that Axtell damage suit next month."

"No reason I can't do that."

He shook his head stubbornly. "It'll take ten days to try. If you get hung up in this you know you won't have the time. I understand you well enough to know that, Don." He shook his head. "And for peanuts. You could do better if the judge appointed you."

"Money isn't all, Jake. I'm not hurting right now."

"I know, I know. But this is another murder case. What would Miss Jo say?"

"She was my client once. She'd understand," I said, not sure of that at all.

"I hear there's some hokum church involved and that they probably aren't going to want you messing in it." He nodded, finding another chink in my armor. "How about if we wind up with a bunch of them on the jury panel for the Axtell case or something else later?"

"I'll have to watch close for that," I said humbly.

He checked his place in the advance sheet and closed it with an annoyed slap. He nodded up at me.

"Well, if you've got to do it, if something comes along where you need some help . . ."

I nodded. "I already need it. I always need it. You know that. I'd like for you to sniff around in your own inimitable way. Somehow you never cause the waves I do."

"That's because I don't try to force things, I try to finesse them."

"Whatever," I said. "I need to depose all of the kids at the welfare house, plus the new couple who took over after the killings, and a man named Bishop Shooken. You're better at paper work than I am. Can you dictate me something so we can get it going real soon? Plus a motion for a speedy trial in case I decide to file one?"

"All right. Do you want me to file the deposition notices and serve them?"

I hesitated just a moment and then nodded. Angler wasn't going to like me.

"Leave the file on my desk and I'll read it. Dictate anything else you have to one of the girls and have her type it up for me. I'll read it when I get back." He looked at his watch. "Right now I'm five minutes late for court." He pointed at the sprawled advance sheet he'd been reading. "Interesting case in that one on hypnotization."

I was two months back on advance sheets. He was punctual. As he went through them weekly he checked things for me to read. Some weekend soon I'd come in and gorge myself with legal reading and catch up.

After he'd gone I dictated what I had to one of the secretaries.

To find Cyclops was easy enough. During the days he racked balls and did cleanup at Eddo's Pool Emporium, which opened late and then remained open until the small hours. It was a dingy place which also sported an upstairs poker game where the stakes were whatever the unwary would approve and the chances of winning extremely remote and hazardous.

Cyclops had been hanging around or working in downtown Bington all the time I'd been a resident of the town. He was a tiny, sunny man in his late thirties with an IQ not doubly higher than that age. He'd never graduated from Bington High School although he'd remained a student there, according to local legend, for a lot of years. Now he dressed like the kids he idolized, talked their talk, passed on their stories, and knew all their gossip. He could fill you in on such varied and interesting things as how many girls in the sophomore class were pregnant, the assorted facts and figures on the B.H.S. football team, who of the teachers was an easy grader and who wasn't. He knew the high school jocks, brains, and party people. He even knew the teachers.

He was useful to the kids and so they had adopted him.

He ran errands, passed messages, and, most important, bought booze for them. The buying sin was widely known and now and then he'd be hauled into court and thereafter pay a fine. Kids who finked on Cyclops, even where duress was severe, were rare and sometimes thereafter found themselves ostracized by their peers. Cyclops himself wouldn't be angry with them, but he was sufficiently intelligent not to make the same mistake twice and to spread the word on defectors.

After an afternoon spent in the office, where I'd closed a mortgage and talked with two prospective divorcees, both of whom had cried, I walked to Eddo's. I found the place cool, dirty as usual, and vacant. Cyclops dusted tables idly. He wore jeans and an old, given or borrowed purple-letter sweater with Bington High's white "B" emblazoned on it.

"Buy you a coffee, Cyclops?"

He nodded carefully at me. We weren't that close, but I'd never been unkind.

I fed coins into a machine and it gave back two plastic cups filled with vile-tasting brew. I split with Cyclops and we retired to folding chairs behind the counter.

"How'd you get that nickname—Cyclops?" I asked, to start it.

"I used to wear real thick glasses," he said. "Now I got me some contacts." He watched me. "You ain't deputying or nothing are you, Donny?" he asked anxiously, unsure of my place in the world of law.

I shook my head.

"One time old Speedball Jeffries did that to me. Came in here and gave me a beer or two and then got me telling stories about who I was buying for." He smiled his happy, vacant smile. "All the time I don't know he's a new sworn deputy. That was a good one on me, wasn't it, Donny?"

"Sure it was," I said, "but not fair."

He waited, knowing I wanted something, eying me shyly and patiently.

"Cyclops, do you know Cherry Rettner?"

He smacked his lips appreciatively. "Sure, man. I know her. She's real pretty. Too bad. Too bad." An unaccustomed frown wrinkled his smooth forehead. Sometimes, when he thought hard, he gave the impression of being in actual physical pain.

"What do you hear about it?" I asked.

He shook his head slowly.

"You got her the knife, didn't you?"

"I loaned her a knife once. She said she needed it. Now they tell around she did real bad things with it, but that them people was ripe and needed it done." He watched me from a faraway place where all decisions came hard. "I guess they needed it for sure, didn't they, Donny?"

"Is that all you hear?"

"That's what the people say. Cherry used to have lots of bumps and bruises."

"Did you ever see any of them?"

"No, not really," he said, looking perplexed. "But she told me she hurt."

"What's Angler saying about it?"

"That Angler's a smart one, Donny. He can do almost anything. The other guys are afraid of him. Even football guys are scared. When Angler says frog they're already hopping. Now he's telling that nothing much bad is going to happen to Cherry."

"And the twins he hangs with? Do they ever say anything?"

He tried hard to remember, but perhaps he'd never known. He shook his head.

"I swear I don't remember nothing about them . . ."

"But you've heard that Angler is telling around that nothing will happen to Cherry?"

"Sure."

"Do you know a Bishop Shooken?"

"No," he said, looking mystified.

"Did you ever buy Cherry any booze?"

"Not her, Donny," he answered anxiously. "If she wanted any I'd just give it to her. I like her."

"But maybe you bought some for the people she runs with? Sam or Kate? Angler and the twins?"

"I know Kate, but I don't know any Sam. Them others you mention are big, mean guys," he said seriously. "I seen them lifting weights once. They could lift both of us and throw us away, too. They dope some, but they don't never drink." He shook his head, concerned. "You stay clear of them. They do evil, bad, nasty stuff. And Angler, he's real smart."

"What kind of bad stuff? You mean bad stuff like burglaries and stealing?"

"That and different from that. They do worse. You know old Mr. Fitzgerald? He used to be a teacher at the high when I was there. He was a teacher for them, too, but he ain't no more." His voice had *almost* pain in it.

"How come?"

"His wife had the bad high blood and she was real sick, sometimes in the hospital, then sometimes at home. When she was home I heard that people kept calling her on the phone and saying dirty things, then left things where she would find them, like dead rats and cats. Then a lot of wasps got into their house. Mr. Fitz, he had a year to go teaching, but he had to quit sudden to take care of her. She died." He nodded severely. "There was other stuff, too. But don't you let on I told you anything, Donny. Them are mean guys, real mean."

"Tell me more about them, Cyclops? Whatever you know?"

He shivered a little and drew away. "Not me," he said, but I could see he wanted to tell me more.

"Come on," I said softly. "I promise I won't tell them anything you say."

"I don't know much. They do about like they want. The other kids don't mess with them. I seen them lifting weights and I guess they do that lots to pass the time. I never bought nothing for them, not anytime. They push and pick, but if they asked, I would. I hear they sell dope at school sometimes. They say that Angler can read a book in half an hour and then say it back to you. A big book, not no comic book. Think of that?" A touch of wistfulness came into his voice. He was just bright enough to know he wasn't bright, but his world was as real to him as mine was to me and perhaps as meaningful.

I had a sudden moment of empathy for him and his narrow world. "That isn't so much, Cyclops. It's only a trick some people can do. I bet he can't play a three-rail shot like you can."

He brightened. He was a good billiards and pool player. It was his life. All that kept him from being a very good one was lack of ability to plan far ahead.

He leaned toward me. Around us the poolroom was silent, but from upstairs I could hear the dim sounds of a card game in progress.

"You're going to get Miss Cherry off, aren't you, Donny?"

"I'm going to do the best I can for her," I said. "Where'd you get the knife you loaned her?"

He shook his head. "One day I sort of found it in my letter sweater. Someone must have give it to me and I forgot maybe." He looked away and I thought there was a good chance he'd stolen it. "Cherry was around when I found it. She wanted to borrow it and so I said that would be okay. I gave it to her."

I nodded.

"I'll listen around for you, Donny. Maybe I'll hear something." He smiled. "Sometimes kids talk a lot and don't even see me. I'll tell you what I hear. I swear it on this letter sweater." He crossed his heart solemnly.

"You be careful while you're listening," I cautioned. He was so guileless that anyone would quickly read his intentions. "Don't ask anyone anything."

"Sure," he said, nodding. "You be real careful, too." He patted me clumsily on the back.

CHAPTER VI

Alcoholic beverages may be sold or dispensed to adults where proper licenses are obtained and displayed by the seller.

I wasn't a Bington native and there were many local names which were still unfamiliar to me, but I knew who Fitzgerald was, even knew his first name was Cecil. He'd appeared at a zoning hearing I'd also attended. He'd ably protested my client's desire to change his home into a business place to sell antiques. I'd lost.

I looked up the ex-client's address and, armed with that, I looked up Cecil Fitzgerald in the city directory after finding no phone listed under his name. His address was near my ex-client's. I drove the LTD out and parked it under a streetlight. It was full dark.

Fitzgerald's house was situated on a small lot near the university. I figured one day soon the house would, by operation of the power of eminent domain, be university land. The house was tiny and square, neatly painted, well kept. All the outside lights were on, but I saw no lights inside. I rang a bell and heard it sound inside. I waited awhile and rang again. When I'd decided that no one would be along the door opened cautiously, still chained in three places.

"Yes?" a voice inquired.

"Mr. Fitzgerald?"

He opened a little wider and I could see tired eyes and a fierce, hooked nose. "That's me," he admitted reluctantly. "I remember you from someplace." He snapped dry, old fingers clumsily. I got a smell of him and could tell he'd had a drink or two.

"I'm Don Robak, Mr. Fitzgerald. Remember me?"

He nodded.

"Just now I'm representing a girl named Cheryl Rettner who's in the local jail on a murder charge. One of the witnesses is a boy named Angler . . ."

"Why bother me about it?" he cut in.

"Your name came up when I was inquiring around about Angler and his twin friends. So I wanted to talk with you about them."

"I don't care about any of those people."

"Could I come in and talk to you?" I asked. "Just for a little while?"

"Wait a minute," he said grudgingly. He closed the door and I heard the chains being undone. In a moment he reopened the door.

"Come in."

I followed him into a dim living room. One tiny bulb glowed, a night light plugged low into the wall. All the curtains were closed tightly. He turned on a table lamp and sat me down in an easy chair.

He was a tiny, combative-looking man, his hook nose making him appear like a hungry bird of prey. He blinked at me in the light.

"I'm sorry," he said. "I still keep everything locked and

I keep it pretty dark in here also. When you leave I'll lock up and turn off the lights again."

"There are the windows," I pointed out.

"Barred. They could get in, but I'd have some warning. More than she had."

"You mean your wife?"

He nodded. "She was already sick. I never could prove a thing. I never saw them, although I tried to catch them. They did things."

"That's why I came. I heard about that."

"You didn't hear all of it. They'd rub the phone and electric wires in two. At nights the water would go off. They used front porch, yard, and my car for their bowel movements. They must have gotten keys somewhere. I'd lock things, but they'd still get in wherever they wanted."

I remembered the locks on the dormitory doors and nodded. Maybe they could get out, but how?

"Nothing was safe," he continued. "Lots of nights I'd hide in the garage with my shotgun. No one would come, but I'd hear them far out in the darkness, laughing, catcalling. They teased her and worried her over the brink she was already near and so she died. She was going to die anyway, but they had no right to hasten it."

"You say *they* did things. Who did them?"

"Your client for one. She was in it along with her boy friends. Sick. She's sick. I never saw her or them, not even one time, but she told me she was going to get me when I flunked her."

"I see. You failed Cheryl Rettner in one of your classes? That's it?"

"She wouldn't do the work. It got to be a personality

thing between us. She was loud and disruptive in class. She told everyone who'd listen that I'd made passes at her. In class she'd cross her legs and hike up her skirt and sit there. I flunked her, Mr. Robak. She was smart enough to pass. I knew she'd pulled the same thing with others and gotten away with it." He shook his head. "She was smart enough to pass if she'd done even a little of the work."

"She's in jail now, Mr. Fitzgerald. She probably will be there for a long time."

"Jail won't hold her. She'll lie her way out and they'll help her. Wait and see. It's all a part of Angler's plans. He's the brains. I had him in class, too. The rest aren't dumb, but he's the planner and he's as twisted as a pretzel. I still don't think they're done with me. Even with this other trouble going on I'm waiting and ready."

"How are you ready?" I asked curiously.

He shrugged, apparently unsure of me. "That's my business, Mr. Robak. Just tell your client next time you talk with her that I'm ready and waiting for them." He nodded. "You do that. Tell her for me."

"How about police? Didn't you call the police when they were bothering your wife?"

"I called dozens of times. I tried everyone, police, sheriff, prosecutor, judge. The police patrolled and watched. They picked them up three or four times and questioned them. Angler spent days in detention. When the police were watching close it would stop or slow down for a while, but it would start up again as soon as they stopped patrolling. And one of the police officers told me that when they were watching there'd be fake calls to the station about fires and break-ins. Angler's quite patient and inventive." He looked at me, the light shining off his nose, his old eyes intent. "Did you ever see a match gun, Mr. Robak?"

"Made from clothes pins?" I asked, remembering a bit of misspent youth.

He nodded. "I see you know about them. That's their newest finding. Angler or one of his cohorts is becoming very good with a match gun. I have to be most careful with combustibles. The other night I'm almost sure they fired my trash sacks. I heard a car go past slow. When I looked out the sacks were on fire, but I was too smart to go out. I think they'd like to catch me out in the open at night. What worries me is that this house is old and it's frame. They could splash gasoline someplace. It could occur to them to burn me out."

"You really believe that?"

He nodded solemnly, a tired old man, slightly mad from the loss of his wife, given a little to drink, and no longer willing to think things through logically.

"And all of this because you gave Cheryl Rettner a failing grade?"

"She warned me," he said plaintively. "I suppose I should have done like the others and just not made waves. I'd sell out and move on to the teachers' home if I wasn't so damned stubborn. This was our house. Ella's house. I just can't leave yet. Maybe I will sell when this is over."

"And will it be over soon?"

"I think so."

"How do they know when you're here alone and that there aren't police around?"

"I've thought about that. For a long time I thought

they had the house bugged, but I never could find anything. They have to have some way of keeping watch. I've racked my brain and walked all over the neighborhood in the light of day, but I'm still not sure how they do it. They're very cunning and smart." He closed his eyes for a moment. "And I'm so old. I sleep a lot. Sometimes I drink too much."

"Did you know the Davidson couple who were killed?"

"I knew him. I knew who she was."

"How did you know him?" I asked.

"It isn't important now."

"Do you know a Bishop Shooken?"

He shook his head.

"Maybe you ought to try talking to the new sheriff?"

He shook his head wearily. "I don't know him. But he's probably like that last one, the one who died, all gold teeth smiling and not a bit of brains."

"This one's smarter. He used to be a state police detective."

"Bington politics," he said. "Talking with you has made me realize I need another drink."

"I don't belong to the new sheriff's political party," I said stiffly.

He looked at his watch and then away from me. He shook his head. When I tried to ask him more questions his answers made it plain I was no longer welcome and that his drinking would be private.

When I'd exited his front door I could hear him quickly rechaining.

I wandered around downtown until I found Bishop Shooken in the Old Barn Bar and Grill, which is a tavern near the courthouse. It's a successful farmers' bar, catering mostly either to those who bring their products in to sell on the local market or come shopping. I used to frequent it much more than I do now. I quit being a regular when I got tired of hearing perpetual stories about crop rotation, the betrayal of man by the good earth, and too much (or too little) rain. Even if I had to walk a little farther for a drink it soon seemed worth it.

Gayle Jenkins was still the bartender. He'd been bartender in the Old Barn for a lot of years and I'd heard he had a piece of the place. He was a big man who'd come to town from a small, rocky farm and who'd once, in a fit of alcohol, confided privately to me that he'd never go back. He could talk land language. These days he affected overalls when working behind his bar, wore what was left of his hair long, and I'd heard that sometimes when off duty he'd whittle while he sat gossiping on the courthouse wall. A man who had every intention of being a success. I knew him pretty well.

He gave me a surprised look when I entered. The crowd was sparse in the huge old bar. From the back of the room, where the tables were hidden in darkness, I could hear a voice I recognized exhorting about the might and the right, interspersing comments about the idiocies of the U. S. Supreme Court.

I'd made myself a bet I'd find him if I wandered around, and, having won, I sat down at the bar. I shook hands with Jenkins and ordered Early Times and water. It came and was a little weak, but these days they all seem that way.

"How you making it, Don? How's crime?" Jenkins asked, wheezing a bit.

"Good enough, Gayle."

I sat on the stool and glanced now and then in the mirror behind the bar, and made conversation with Jenkins. In a little while Shooken appeared behind me.

"You following me?" he asked, low-voiced.

"Should I be?"

He shook his massive head suspiciously. "I've never seen you in here before."

Behind the bar Jenkins ignored us.

"I used to come in here real often," I said. "Maybe I'll start again."

"I don't want you trailing me or bothering me, Robak."

I smiled. "I come in here for my own purposes. I assume you do the same."

He frowned severely. "Men who drink a lot need to know about the devil, Mr. Lawyer. That's why I come into places like this."

"I've heard you were a very good man at frequenting them." I waved at Jenkins for another drink. "Care to join me?"

"Never with you, Mr. Lawyer. I don't drink for fun. It's part of my work."

"Now that I've sort of wandered onto you, Mr. Shooken, I had a few questions I wanted to ask you. It could save us both time if I asked them now."

He shook his head and his voice came up. "My title is Bishop Shooken. And I doubt I could or would do anything, say anything, which could help you with that little hellion."

"But such a pretty little girl," I protested.

He nodded at me. "Women like her have caused the wars, passed on the diseases of shame, and murdered their lovers down ten thousand years, Robak. I have been given an ability to sometimes ferret them out."

"Did you do any ferreting on her before the killings? Like maybe when she was in one of her spells?"

"No," he said. "No sir, I did not."

I remembered something Jake had earlier said in our offices, something about a case in the advance sheets he wanted me to read. An idea came.

"I'm considering having her hypnotized so she can remember the whole thing. Maybe I'll do it soon, maybe I'll wait until right up at trial time to do it." I nodded at his white hair and dark face. "Ought to be both effective and interesting."

He watched and waited, but I imagined I saw something change in his eyes.

"She was sick, Mr. Shooken."

"Again, my title is Bishop."

I shook my head. "Not to me, Mr. Shooken. That little girl is sick with a brain disease."

"Yes," he agreed solemnly. "A sickness to pass on to all she touched or touches."

"Weren't you one of those she touched?" I asked, leaning close, keeping my voice low. "That night?"

He raised a huge hand and pushed at me. He was enormously strong. "No more of your slander, Robak." His eyes were almost unseeing. "No more of you."

"She told me things," I lied.

"She hasn't told you the truth," he said. "It's her word against mine." He turned away, his face agitated. "Don't follow or come near me again. Don't even talk to me if you value yourself."

"I'm going to depose you, Mr. Shooken. I'm going to

make you lie under oath. I know you were there that night."

I said it to his back. He was walking away.

It was late and I'd had no dinner. I could go past the downtown Moose and have something there, but that would mean questioning from Marla Rettner. I was more tired than hungry and I thought maybe the Reds were playing the Braves on the tube. So I drove home.

Home was a shotgun apartment where I lived (mostly) alone. It was one of two in an old, remodeled house. The Coulsons lived next door, but they were older people, usually off somewhere on a trip, winters in Florida, summers visiting their kids all over the country.

I parked the LTD in front and went up on my porch, fumbling for the key. Children played kick the can with the can spotted under the solitary, moth-picketed streetlight at the corner. One small boy, maybe ten years old, watched me nervously from where he hid near the edge of my porch.

"Shhhh," he implored. "Don't let on to Mickey that I'm here and I'll tell you something in return."

"Sure," I agreed, not looking at him.

"There's a hole behind this bush. It opens to under your porch," he confided. "Mickey'll never find me. And I can see everything. Sooner or later he'll have to go the other way and I can get in and kick it."

"Good luck," I said, fumbling for my key.

"That ain't it. There's also a guy watching out from that abandoned house up the street. You know, the one they've been working on," he said.

I knew the one he meant. It had stood empty for several years, part of an estate. Recently someone had bought it.

"Watching? Watching what?"

"I don't know. Maybe just watching. I was in there and he run me off mean. Big guy."

"With lots of muscles?"

"Yep."

I put the key in my lock, thinking about it. Nothing to do. Let them watch.

By the porch the boy suddenly took off at a furious pace for the can beneath the light. I watched enviously as he kicked it into the outer darkness and scampered away.

I went inside my apartment. There were eggs in the icebox. I scrambled three and cooked them in butter and ate them with toast. I checked my window locks and bolted the front door and then put a kitchen chair under the knob.

There was no baseball game on television, but there was a Western with a pretty saloon girl and a lot of fast guns. I watched that for all of fifteen minutes before I fell asleep.

When the phone rang I thought it might be my girl, Jo, but it wasn't. The voice was male and deep, no voice I'd ever heard. An angry voice.

"Is this here Lawyer Robak?"

"Yes."

"This is a good friend to the Davidsons. They had lots of friends and we're still their friends even if they are murdered. We know about you, Lawyer Robak. We know crooked lawyers can mess things up. If you do that this time you're going to hurt for it both in this world and the next one."

"Identify yourself," I said. "Then maybe we can discuss it face to face."

That got only a laugh. "You mess this around, you do anything you oughtn't do, and you'll find out right quick who we are."

"You tell Bishop Shooken I figured out quick who put you up to calling," I said, but it was, of course, too late. I was talking to a buzzing phone. I hung up. I was a little angry, but not greatly alarmed. I'd had a lot of phone calls down the years, calls that threatened, late calls that came like chills in the night. I'd had calls offering money and political preference and calls that had hinted darkly about my future health and safety.

I slept well enough. There was one dream where a man appeared, all in white, and offered to show me the way.

My only problem, in the dream, was he kept pointing the way with a gun.

I awoke from that one sweating, but managed to get back asleep quickly enough.

CHAPTER VII

A child is a dependent child if before his or her eighteenth birthday such child's physical or mental condition is endangered by neglect of any kind whatsoever.

In the morning, sleepy-eyed, I walked up from my apartment to the house where they were working, the one where the boy had reported the watcher. I went inside. I was early enough to be there before the workmen. I explored through the house and soon found the place where I thought he'd been. I could see where a saw horse had been moved away from a window and there were half a dozen tiny cigarette roaches stamped blackly against the floor. I lifted one and sniffed carefully. My untrained nose told me nothing. I found an old bank-receipt paper in my wallet and scraped all the remains into it.

I went back outside. The day was lovely, without a hint of rain. I decided to walk. I found it was a fortunate thing I'd made such a decision. All four tires on my LTD were down so that it sat flatly against the pavement. I checked the tires. If they'd been slashed I couldn't find the cuts. More likely a puncture tool of some kind. *Notice me. See my power.*

I went inside my apartment and called my nearby filling station. I was promised a look before noon.

Outside again, I checked the house for other damage and found some. All of my flowers had been ripped out of their beds and strewn here and there about the yard. That made me even angrier. I wondered who'd done it—my watcher or my caller, or both perhaps?

I walked to the office. On the way I stopped at Mac's Grill, where I had coffee black, hot cakes, and discussed the Reds' baseball with a disgruntled local banker. The Reds had lost again last night and the banker was having a very cool morning toward management. He had me nodding in agreement with his logic, but he sent me mortgages now and then and I was still angry about my tires and flowers.

"No bunt, no win," he said harshly to my back as I paid my bill and headed out Mac's door.

Kate awaited me. I'd forgotten about her. She came from behind a tree and confronted me.

"It's getting pretty late," she complained. "They'll wonder where I am." She'd encased her thin body in jeans and a T-shirt.

"Who'll wonder?"

"All of them, Mr. Robak. When I left I saw Bishop Shooken coming. That means there'll be a good breakfast. He brings eggs and stuff."

"When we get done inside I'll spring for enough for pancakes and sausage for you if you want," I said. "Why does Shooken spend so much time out there at the welfare house?"

"I don't know for certain. I'm pretty sure he owns the house, but that might not be his reason."

"The house doesn't belong to welfare?"

She shook her thin, lank hair. "No. I think maybe he owns it and rents it to welfare some way. At least he's always poking around in the house—you ain't safe no place from him. He gets all he can and he don't do a thing for repairs. That window in my room's been out since the night Cherry went bonkers. He's never even tried to fix it. He's too cheap." She nodded. "Angler told Cherry and she told me that Shooken has lots of places, rentals, houses sold on contracts, houses where he's taken mortgages or pledged money." She smiled. "While he's stealing from you he talks real pleasant."

"You go to this place where he has his services?"

"Sure. We get made to go. First by the Davidsons and now by the Allens. That old man raises hell about almost everything. He particularly don't like lawyers like you. Somehow going out there don't bother Angler. He goes willing and makes the twins come too. Lots of people there. Noise and music. Sometimes hundreds of people."

"Why does Shooken hate Cherry so much?"

She gave me a surprised look. "Does he?"

I nodded. "He starts foaming at the mouth every time her name gets mentioned."

She looked away. "I don't know for sure. He always got on with her before the Davidsons died. Now and then he'd be around when she had a spell." She shook her head. "There's lots I don't know from out there, Mr. Robak. They didn't let us out much nights."

We walked on to the jail.

Sheriff Abe wasn't in evidence, but Woodrow London, a deputy I knew well, was on the desk. He was a grumbler and a mumbler. For a time he'd patrolled the roads for previous sheriffs, but if trouble occurred in east county Woodie was always in west county. If there was a problem in the north you could bet you couldn't raise Woodie on the radio until he was in the deep south. A cautious man. Also a man who knew where many political bodies lay buried and how to exhume them. Woodie had hung grimly on through four sheriffs now, pension shining far back in his eyes. Sheriff Abe had at least put him where he could be of some use and where he could be watched.

In deference to Kate, grumbling about it all the way, he led us up back steps and into a special entrance to the juvenile detention area. By going that way we didn't have to pass the adult area, but it was still early and I could hear nothing of the curser.

The inside of the jail smelled like coffee brewed mostly of dust and urine.

I stood away and watched the reunion. The girls shrieked incoherently at each other, touched hands through the bars, cried, and then fell into soft, animated conversation. They kept their voices low so it was difficult for me to hear. I could tell it was mostly catching up about Sam and Angler and the twins. When there was something they wanted strictly private they merely put their heads together while I stood watching uncomfortably.

I waited. After a time they seemed to have taken care of the most pressing of their dealings and so I could get in some questions of my own.

"Did Dr. Buckner come here to examine you?" I asked Cherry.

She nodded, not too happy about it. "He came late yesterday."

"Tell me about it."

"He asked a lot of questions and made some doodles on a pad. He used a light to look in my eyes and ears and he tapped me and touched me and then asked a whole bunch more questions. I don't think he much believed my story."

"How'd you like to maybe make him truly believe it?"

"I don't understand."

"I've been considering trying to get someone to hypnotize you. Maybe, that way, you could remember everything which took place that night."

She shook her head.

"Does the thought of being hypnotized bother you?"

"I don't know. I got bad head problems and I've always had them. Sometimes I feel like I'm just barely hanging on. I'd want to think hard and consult with my friends on a thing like being hypnotized." She watched me. Suddenly there were bright tears in her eyes and I wondered where they'd come from and why. "What would happen if we did that and I started mumbling a lot of things I shouldn't?" She shook her head. "No. This is my life. I don't want to be no experiment." She looked at me. "You don't believe me either, do you?"

"Of course," I lied. "It was just something I was thinking about. A place to run to maybe." Out of the corner of my eye I could see that Kate had moved away so that our conversation was private as long as our voices remained low.

"Well I ain't going to do it."
"Okay."
She waited.
"Has anyone else been in to see you?"
"Only Mr. Leaks, the prosecutor. He said he just wanted to make sure everything was all right." She nodded. "And he also asked me some questions about my medicine. I think maybe he took samples with him."
I nodded. "What did you tell him?"
"I told him he'd have to talk to you."
"Good for you. How'd you find out about him taking some of your medicine?"
"They bring the whole bottle up when it's time for my pills. I keep count. I could see several pills were gone." She shook her head. "That Mr. Leaks, he's after me hard, isn't he?"
"It's his job," I said.
"No. It's more than that somehow to him. To hell with him, Mr. Robak."
Kate appeared beside me as Cherry's voice rose. "You do what Mr. Robak tells you. Him and Angler will get you off."
Cherry nodded. "Angler sent in word that you'd been out messing around the welfare house."
"How'd he do that?" I asked. "Get word in?"
"Angler's got lots of ways," Cherry said, smiling at my question. "Someone has to bring in food, deliver stuff, give out fresh bedding, take prisoners in and out of here. Angler knows lots about how jails operate." She nodded. "Angler knows lots about everything."
"I think he knows how to let air out of tires," I said. "And he's a bad gardener."

"He don't do jokes without reason," she said righteously.

"Maybe. Maybe not. Do you and Angler know a retired teacher named Fitzgerald?"

"Where'd you get his name?" she asked, concerned. "Who told you about that old mouse, Fitzgerald?"

"I've got my ways also," I said.

"I had him as a teacher once," she said. "He was mean and dirty, an old man, always peeking and patting and pinching."

"And so?" I asked, not believing her.

"And so he made Angler mad. Angler was in his class, too. It ain't bright to make Angler mad." She looked up at me, trying to explain. "You got to understand Angler, Mr. Robak. It's important to my case. Angler gets mad and it can get very bad. He keeps getting madder and madder."

"Why'd Angler get mad at Fitzgerald in the first place?"

"It was something at school."

"It was about you, wasn't it, Cherry?"

"It sort of began that way. Maybe it never would have gone any further, but Fitzgerald is kind of like Angler. He made it personal with Angler. He came sneaking out around the welfare house and said things to the Davidsons. He brought Davidson a big box of whiskey and they drank together. Davidson used to phone him now and then after that." She shook her head. "Nobody should make things personal with Angler."

"Maybe Davidson and his wife made it personal with Angler, too? Is that it? Are there things about this you know and aren't telling me? Maybe Angler was out of his room the night the Davidsons died?"

"He was locked in. Ask the twins or Sam or Kate, here. Ask the sheriff." She shook her head wearily. "It was me, Mr. Robak. I did it."

"You're not sure one way or the other. You were in a spell, a fit, blacked out for a long time. At least that's what you've told me up to now. Are you changing that?"

Kate tugged at my sleeve. "Angler didn't do nothing that night, Mr. Robak." Her eyes were fearful. "I'd have heard."

Cherry nodded agreement and leaned close to the bars. Her look was intense. "Angler likes you, Mr. Robak. He thinks you're smart. He sent word in there were a few small problems, but he was sure it would work out." She smiled. "Please see it does. Angler can help." The words were almost a plea.

"I have to know how he can help," I said. "I've been in the legal business for a long time. I think I know how to do things."

"It just can't be your way if Angler don't think so," she said. I could see fear in her eyes. She nervously shook her yellow curls, seeing I was unconvinced. She tried another tear or two, but I waited silently until she'd dried her eyes.

"I run my own show," I said. "Juveniles, age seventeen and under, make no decisions for me. I make them all myself." I examined her, having said the words to see what effect they'd cause. She seemed convinced that Angler was always right and I didn't want it that way. I was almost surely going to have to make Angler look like a possible murderer in the upcoming trial, an alternative.

I said, "For me to get you off I've got to show there

were other possibilities. I need to do my homework to manage that. It's your only chance, Cherry."

Her eyes didn't waver. "Please, Mr. Robak."

"If it can't be the way I say then I'd best not be in your case."

She looked down at the floor and nodded, resigned to what I was saying, agreeing with it.

"A lawyer's a lawyer," she whispered softly. "Angler told me that."

"Angler tells you almost everything," I said roughly. "I think you'd better have someone representing you who can do just exactly what Angler says until you either get your life term or your death penalty."

Kate was watching us, her face stricken. "Don't fire Mr. Robak, Cherry." She looked imploringly at me. "She don't mean nothing. She's just scared."

"I want you to stay on," Cherry said coolly, still not looking directly at me. "But would you please tell Angler what the doctor tells you about me? And maybe there ought to be more doctors."

"More doctors? Sure. And I'll tell Angler when I depose him." I watched for further reaction, but there was none. Maybe Angler's opposition to depositions hadn't been communicated to her yet. "The office is making up papers for depositions now. They may be already done and to the next step. Next time Angler sends in word or you send word out you can tell him I'll let him know exactly what's happening at the time I depose him."

Watching her, I couldn't tell whether Angler had told her anything about his instructions to me on depositions. If he had she gave no overt sign. He probably hadn't, I decided. After all, hadn't he already issued his orders to me?

"Tell me what your relationship with Bishop Shooken has been."

She looked slightly surprised. "We go out there to meetings. The Davidsons made us go there. The bishop and Angler talk some."

"How about you and Bishop Shooken? Did he ever talk to you?"

She shrugged. "He was around a lot. I could see him watching me now and then. You know, the way men do."

"Did he ever try to do more?"

"No. I don't know. Maybe he did. For a while, when I'd have a spell, when the medicine stopped, the Davidsons would get him there to try to run off my demons. I can remember him vaguely being there when the attacks weren't real bad."

Downstairs I spied the sheriff in his office. I gave Kate money for breakfast and sent her on her way and waited amiably in front of the sheriff's desk until he noticed me.

"You're up at it early," he said.

"I'm a citizen come to make a complaint," I explained.

He smiled, refusing to understand, so I smiled back. It was his job and his jail and right now I needed his good will. The years have taught me to be a chameleon.

"Riddle me a few answers, Abe. What would make those boys out at the welfare home put a watch on me?"

"Are they doing that?" he asked, mildly interested.

I nodded. "Someone in my neighborhood spotted one of the twins watching from a house being repaired up the street from where I live. I went up there this morning and gathered this." I handed him the paper with the residues in it. "And apparently those same boys have made life very difficult for a retired teacher named Cecil Fitzgerald. Know him?"

He shook his head.

"Nice enough old man, but they've run him to the brink of the bughouse with about every dirty trick that nasty, inventive young minds can think of."

"Kid stuff," he scoffed.

"More than that. A lot more. His wife probably died as a result of some of the kid stuff." I moved in a little closer. "And after being watched last night somehow all four tires on my car were flat this morning, plus my flowers were pulled out of their beds."

"Did you see who did it?"

"No."

"Then I'd like to be of service, Don, but today I've got half a ton of court papers to serve, plus jurors to call for jury duty next week. I'm still looking into a dozen break-ins, including that one where all the necessities for a dynamite party were taken. So if there are kids doing something inside the city limits of Bington which they oughtn't to do you take it to the city boys and not me. It's their jurisdiction. They've even got some specially trained juvenile officers down there." He smiled at me. "A whole covey of them to chase your mean kids, write up reports about it, and appear upstairs when his honor holds his sometimes juvenile hearings."

"If that welfare house you sent me to the other day is in the county then those kids live in the county."

"The house is in the county, but what kids do in town is Bington's business. And if such kids are smoking this then that also is city business."

"You're already developing a lazy streak," I said easily. "Maybe it's the chair you occupy."

"Not lazy, friend. Overworked. I finally got to sleep sometime after two this morning." He nodded at me, his eyes earnest. "Did you ever lay awake and try to figure out what was going to happen with almost a full case of dynamite? That's what's bugging me. Someone set off a few sticks up north. We got calls on an explosion, but we haven't found exactly where it was set off yet. Someone maybe trying it for size. What's killing me and the federal man who stayed around is what's going to go down with the rest of it." He shook his head dolefully. "Go tell your troubles to the city. And take your probable pot with you."

My relationship with the Bington department was now at a low ebb. "Can't I talk you into at least a field test?"

"I suppose I could do that." He rummaged through a drawer and found a field test kit. It's a plastic affair. You insert the suspected sample and then mix it with a liquid chemical which is already in the kit. There's a color change to purple or black if the sample is marijuana. I've heard police officers say it isn't a hundred per cent test, but it's widely used.

I watched. He worked the plastic around and in a while we had a result. It came to a medium purple.

"Probably home grown. Ten per cent of the kids in town are growing their own in secluded areas, then selling the crop to the other ninety per cent." He grinned. "Cheaper that way, less expensive than booze even."

I wondered where my watching friends were growing theirs.

"One more thing, Abe. The night the Davidsons were killed you said you got a call on it. Male or female caller?"

He shook his head. "Damned if I know. Could have been either. Maybe a handkerchief across the phone to muffle up things. Someone who maybe heard the screaming from the road and didn't want to get involved. Some of those neighbors out there hate that place and complain about it every chance they get."

CHAPTER VIII

The term of office for judges of the circuit court in this state shall be six years.

Outside the sun was now high enough for me to tell it was going to be another fine, warm day. I walked on to my office and tried to call Dr. Buckner, but he wasn't in and his nurse was vague about how I could run him down once I admitted I wasn't in immediate danger of death. I left word for him to call or get in touch.

I called Bington's welfare department. I was shunted here and there and finally wound up talking with a lady I knew, but of whom I'd lost track. She was properly suspicious of me on the phone, crisply informed me that her day was already far too crowded to see the likes of me, then grudgingly gave me an appointment for later that afternoon, when I insisted.

I hung around the office for a time, but Jake didn't appear. One of the secretaries told me she thought he was in city court.

I therefore did what I'd been wanting to do for a while.

I walked back to the courthouse to see Judge Steinmetz.

It was difficult for me to envision a courthouse without Steinmetz, but next year it was going to be that way.

Through the vagaries of the political infighting of the ruling party he'd been defeated in the primary.

"What will you do?" I'd asked, when I'd first heard.

"Well, I can sit around home and maybe read the labels in my suit coats on bad days. On good days I could walk down to the river and then walk back up from the river. Harold Emsden, the baker, said I could come past his place and watch the dough rise. I could observe them cutting hair at the barber shop. But maybe I'll write my memoirs, including a hot section on you. Lots of interesting stuff, Robak."

Getting no help from him, I'd asked around about how he'd gotten beaten. The lawyer who'd done it was a callow youth, unfit to carry Steinmetz's shoes. I'd heard he'd run in the first place only to get his name known.

"It was him getting messed up in that last teachers' strike," one confidante commented darkly.

Another incorrectly said, "He got soft on juvenile things."

A third: "He quit coming to party doings."

And another: "He didn't do one single bit of campaigning."

Later, catching him in a better mood, I did get out of Steinmetz that he was tired and so he'd just not fought. He seemed undisturbed at his defeat.

I skirted the downstairs brass spittoons (which Frieda, the dainty county treasurer, had recently petitioned the commissioners to use as flower pots) and took the creaking elevator to floor four. There, I told Marge, his court reporter, that I'd like to see the man.

"I think he's been expecting you," she said, low-voiced. "He came out yesterday and asked if you'd called or been around recently."

He must have heard us for he appeared at his door, peering around with his slightly slanted eyes. He was a man who always looked as if he'd bitten into a lemon and was surprised and perplexed about the sour taste he'd found.

"Quit conspiring against me," he ordered us. "I hear both of you and I know what you're doing." He grinned and scratched at his bald, old dome. "Come inside, Robak."

Marge smiled encouragingly at both of us. "Come back and conspire some other day, Don."

I followed Steinmetz into his office. His desk was heaped high with papers.

He sat down and faced me.

"I guess I'll be representing Cheryl Rettner," I said. "At least right now I'm representing her."

"You seem uncertain of your circumstances," he said, frowning.

"She has other people she listens to for her advice. Nonlawyers. We may soon come to a parting of the ways because of that."

"I imagine I know of whom you speak." He dug into his redoubtable memory. "A large lad named Angler. It was Angler who once, in a juvenile hearing, demanded bond, a trial by jury, and some hotshot, upstate lawyer he'd heard about to defend him. I gave him none of those things. He runs with a set of twins, all three together making up about half a ton of muscle. Out there at their place of abode would also be a black boy named Sam, who once had the reputation of being a first-class burglar. Then there's a girl named Kate James, a poor, small victim of an unfortunate childhood, a girl who's maybe lucky to be here."

"How's that on Kate?"

"Oh, she's not sick or anything. But all her brothers and sisters wound up damaged in some way. Kate somehow survived whole."

I nodded. "Tell me about how all those kids got out in that home? And why would a gentleman who calls himself Bishop Shooken be acting like the ramrod of the whole thing where they live?"

"Those kids got out there mainly because I sent them there. Each one of those young people has been in this court. As to Mr. Bishop Shooken, he's a man of the finest whole cloth." He winked. "I think he took such cloth when he discovered that churches are exempt from such harassing things as state, local, and federal taxes. I'm surprised you don't know him very well as he wanders in and out of Bington's taverns. There, he preaches about the evils of drink and rescues the poor sots he finds around him during those visits. Some of our local tavern owners have tried to order him out, but he then visits those taverns with lots of help. So most have learned to put up with him. Once he rescues someone he then takes them to his quote, church, unquote, where he fleeces them by kind words and the rapid buying and selling of real estate. He's a master at that. They tell around, and I believe, that Mr. Bishop Shooken can write better contracts to buy and sell off the top of his head than you and I, with all our books and forms, can dictate. I had him in my court once. Some farmer sued him on a land transaction. I wrestled with the case for a time, long enough to draw an anonymous telephone call or two, but couldn't figure out a way to decide it for the farmer, more's the pity. A solid contract." He shook his head. "Shooken came to Bington ten years ago. I've heard, but have never seen evidence, that he was disbarred as a lawyer in another state." He looked away from me and out his window, assessing the traffic in the busy street below. "Perhaps only a rumor spread by his enemies."

I waited, but that seemed to be all he was going to tell me about Shooken.

"How about the kids?" I asked.

"I assume you've done your work and know all about your client so I'll skip her."

"I know almost nothing about her. Her sister hired me. I know a little bit about their relationship. Other than that and the fact that Cheryl is charged with murder, I know very little."

He nodded slowly. I could almost see him running things through the computer behind his eyes. He had a fantastic and unbelievable memory. Each day of his life and each fact acquired was an individual, catalogued thing to him. He seemed never confused and those who checked him out always came back amazed. I'd never known him to be wrong on a checkable fact. A glorious gift, but it could also be fearful. When one remembers one first remembers the times for sorrow. For Steinmetz the times of joy, to balance the bad times, had been few in the past ten years. He'd lost his wife and the days of her dying had been long and filled with pain. A daughter had vanished into the maw of the industrial city to the north and he never spoke of her now. Perhaps she also was gone. There'd been vague stories about drugs. There'd been other family deaths so that now the judge alone, of all his generation, survived. Sometimes he could drown things in icy martinis, forget all for a time, but chronic ulcers made those times few. He was a mediocre but fanatic golfer, and a stunning card player. He had all the patience one could stand to see with young lawyers coming timidly into his court. He had little for us older fumblers. He could occasionally forgive us our incompetences, but he could not silently abide them. He cordially and publicly hated the prosecutor, Herman Leaks, but even Leaks had never claimed Steinmetz was unfair.

He shook his head.

"I think I'll forgo the experience of telling you what I know about your client. If I did so I might somehow indicate a future attitude toward her. Her situation is something you must dig into yourself."

I nodded. "All right. How about the others out there?"

He nodded, pleased I'd not protested his exclusion of Cherry.

"The new tenants," he said, "are Hiram and Alice Allen. He's farmed and sharecropped farms all his life. His last place was the Rondell Pickett farm out on Flower Ridge. He had that one three years and last year they say it came up mostly weeds. As a farmer he seems to suffer from a terminal case of black thumb. Nice enough little man, but ineffectual, no stick-to-it, no get-up-and-go. Spends his time dreaming and talking. But Rev. Shooken has big pull with welfare. He must have got Hiram on, maybe for a lion's share of the profits." He sighed gustily. "Hiram and Alice ought to know some about kids, though. They had six of them, all of them fair enough kids, and all grown and out of the house now. Let's see, there's Hiram, Jr. He's up in Detroit, got a good job there at one of the auto plants, Ford maybe. Wayne's a policeman in Indianapolis. Sydney sells Chevies here—you know him, Don. Then there were the three girls." He meandered on, spelling out who each girl had married, number and gender of children. I sighed and listened. With Steinmetz you accepted the useless with the useful.

When he finally fell silent on the Allens, I reminded, "How about the kids out there?"

"All right. Take the twins, first off. Joe and Jack Shallito. Their parents got killed in a foggy big one out on the interstate. Ran under a stalled semi. The boys were asleep in the back seat. Didn't get a scratch, but they were about three hours sawing them out of the car. They would have been eleven at the time, seventeen now. Since the accident they've been nothing but trouble. One steals and the other lies for him. They like to bully people, start fights, but they aren't expert at it. Very strong, but not very fast. And not real bright, either. Before they went out to the welfare home and Angler took them in his masterful hand they used to get in lots of stupid trouble, mean things, apparent crimes. I had them in front of me about every time we had juvenile hearings." He shook his head sadly. "I've got a sort of inner belief about those two. If their parents hadn't died in that accident, and if the kids hadn't been there to see it and live through it, I think they'd have wound up just regular kids, played football for Bington High, maybe even gone on to college. But something traumatic and lasting happened to them in that car, the blood of their parents all over them, not able to get out, screaming and crying."

"What sort of trouble got them out there to the welfare house?"

"Nothing particular that I know about. They just drifted out there, never stole anything big, never hurt anyone badly. On their own I don't think they have the capacity for big trouble, to think on it, plan it through. They aren't stupid, Don, but they also aren't inventive."

"Angler is," I said.

He nodded. "Oh yes. That's his real last name. George Burton Angler is the full handle. Remember when they were building the big power plant ten miles south? Angler's father was an engineer on it. His mother was a big, healthy girl out of Kentucky. Wandered in here and took up with the engineer, then married him. After the marriage broke up she sang around here. Handsome woman with a fair voice. I heard her once. Untutored, country-western stuff. With a break she might have made it big and I think she dreamed of that. Maybe Angler was in the way and cramped her style. I know the engineer was. She ran him off. He tried to get custody of the boy, but she won out. Some other judge heard it, not me. I'd have given it to him. He got killed about a year later on the job. There was some money and, of course, there was Social Security. By that time things weren't going so good with Momma Angler's career. She was heavy into pills, singing and drinking here and there all over this end of the state, any place that would have her. There were men and more men. She squandered what she got and what Angler got, stole the money his father had left. She should have been sent to prison for it, but no one ever tried. When the local police first started picking Angler up it was because he'd left a home that was cold, deserted, and without food. She'd come get him." He looked up at me. "You know, of course, that when they pick up a juvenile usually they turn him over to his parents and then schedule them in after that for conferences and hearings. Momma Angler never showed for even one hearing. Always an excuse. She'd send him by himself. I remember him from then, bright and defiant. After a time she stopped even coming to pick him up from jail. I tried him in a foster home or two, but nothing worked. He beat another kid up badly, laid in wait for him, so I had to send him on to corrections. When they let him out they placed him out where he is now, not me. He gets picked up these days we report it to their parole officer and he takes care of it."

"Who's their parole officer?"

"Various people. That's one of the problems. We report and nothing happens." He nodded. "Angler's smart, very smart, and I think he's now completely amoral, Don. Someday he'll kill someone. He has a very bad temper."

"He hated the dead couple," I said.

Steinmetz shrugged. "Your problem, not mine."

"How bright is he?"

"Really bright. We've got a file on him here. Brighter than he has any right to be. He thinks no one is smart enough to catch him. Sociopathic personality of course. More and more of them all the time, but Angler's outstanding."

"Maybe he figured out an ingenious way to kill his keepers and get the job blamed on someone else," I said.

"Again, your problem. I only know what the papers filed against Cheryl Rettner say. It's my case, but I haven't had to do much about it yet. Find something for me to do if you want." He smiled at me, a man with just a bit more than half a year left to serve on the bench, still interested and eager. I'd get no special favors from him and I knew him well enough to expect none. He wasn't made that way. He'd sit here with me and talk, but he'd do the same for almost anyone.

"Would you want to have her arraigned?" he asked genially. "Any morning from nine to ten is open. Shouldn't take a lot of time. We could attempt to work out a trial date then, too."

"Very soon I'll need to do that," I said, not yet ready. "Tell me about the other two kids out there?"

"The black boy is Sam Warf. His mother drifted in from Chicago twelve years back. She lived with Pecky Chasp, remember him?"

I shook my head.

"Pecky wasn't Sam's father. I don't know who that was. Pecky was a second-rate boxer. Got shot in a daylight robbery over at the Valu-Mart six years ago come July. A mean man. He used to smack Sam around some, but the mother did the best she could for him during that time. When Pecky got killed she just sort of quit existing. They had to commit her. I had the hearing. She just sat there, not moving, not doing anything. I ask about her now and then when I have my hearings at the state hospital. She's still there." He shook his head. "They tell me she always will be. The only thing young Sam ever stole in his break-ins was food. He's a food fanatic, knows about it, reads and studies, cooks. He sure loves food even if he looks like he never ate a bite. He gets old enough I'm going to try getting him on in a job someplace where they'll treasure him." He nodded. "Good kid, Don, sensitive and smart. No relatives here and nothing turned up through Chicago. We put him out there because there wasn't any other place." He smiled, perhaps remembering Sam. "I'll bet he's never in a bit of trouble once he makes it up to the magic portal of eighteen years old."

"And Kate?"

"She's smart, too. Not as smart as Angler, maybe, but not twisted as bad as him either. She comes from a family of maybe a dozen. They lived like animals on a farm back in those rough hills near Rooster Run Road. Welfare got into it when the kids didn't go to school. That was a long time ago. Welfare eventually took all the kids. Some went here, some there. Bad news kids. I never heard what happened to the parents afterward. Just drifted on probably. They were squatting on the land. It's hard for me to figure where Kate's brains came from, but she's got them. Maybe someone sneaked in on her daddy. We tried her in foster homes for a time, but she was a problem. Couldn't get along, didn't trust anyone. A loner. Hated her brothers and sisters. She's better now. A lot of bad things happened to her very young, when she was still out there on Rooster Run. She has little trust for anything or anyone. She used to run off lots, but not recently." He shook his head. "I remember the pictures they introduced of the place where they picked up all those kids. A lean-to, low shelves on the walls, the kids sleeping in shifts. There was evidence of sexual abuse. They were made to steal food and raid garbage cans. Ugly memories for Kate. I hope that one day she'll get beyond those times, forget them."

"She likes Cherry. I took her in to see Cherry in jail. They're friends." I remembered the scene.

"That's good," he said approvingly. "Friendship was once beyond her capacity. It was too complicated a relationship for a loner."

"She reads a lot. She was reading when I first saw her."

"She was eight when the welfare took her and she couldn't read a word."

"I thought we were beyond that sort of thing."

He looked away from me and over at his wall. On that wall there were photos of the famous and near famous, most of them standing with Steinmetz, arms locked, smiling friendly smiles.

"We live close on each other, Don. Deviate from the norm and someone usually reports it. The problem is with those places where reports go. They're overworked and understaffed. Sometimes I think we could get at kids with problems and help them if we got there early enough. By the time I get a child in court most of his or her behavior patterns have been set. I can punish and lecture, but I can't change anyone." He shook his head. "I'll be glad to shed the responsibility. Right now I've got a prosecutor who hasn't filed a waiver petition asking to try a juvenile as an adult during his whole term. Angler should be in a maximum security prison and not out there in that welfare home or in some boys' school." He shrugged once more and smiled only a little. "But as I say, he's not really my problem."

A question occurred to me. "What happened to Angler's mother?"

"Last I heard she was still around town. Try the Jukebox Tavern or Steffi's or one of those places down along the levee."

"Angler said she was dead," I confided. "He said she died when he was eleven years old."

"That would have been about the time she quit getting him released from jail to her. Maybe for him she did die then."

CHAPTER IX

Each county welfare department shall make semiannual reports to the state concerning expenditures, number of persons served, types of aid given, and...

When I exited the front door of the courthouse I found I'd again acquired a watcher. One of the Shallito twins sat on the courthouse wall. He stood out from the crowd of wall sitters because of his age and build, a young bull among old cattle. I smiled at him and nodded as I walked past, but he ignored me. The sun was out and bright. When I was a little way past him I saw him mop his forehead, hop off the wall, and fall in behind.

I walked to the welfare office. Inside there was a long procession of chairs. The room was vacant of waiters except for one old lady who sat hunched in a hard chair near the reception window. She nodded genteelly at me and continued talking to herself.

"Nasty bastards," she said, loud enough for me to hear.

"Who?" I asked. She looked away.

I moved on up to the reception window and tapped. That got an annoyed and harassed glance from a black-haired girl who was typing furiously.

Behind me the old lady decided in my favor. "All of

them," she said. "All these welfares. Thieves and bastards."

"Is that the way it is?" I asked, turning to her.

She wore a dirty cloth coat, far too warm for the day. She was seventyish.

"Have you come for your food stamps? Everyone gets them but me. I stand in their lines, but I don't get that first thing. Bastards all." She nodded positively and crossed her arms. "I'm going to outwait them."

The black-haired girl arose from her typewriter and opened the window an inch.

"Yes?" she asked. She looked me over and added a grudging "Sir?"

I knew really well only one person in the welfare office, although I'd had some early years in the practice when I suppose I'd fit within their financial guidelines for aid. Two years before I'd dated a welfare lady, all very tentative, breaking away before either of us moved to bad habits. A nice girl, one who talked much about her job, dedicated. She was the one I'd called.

"I've an appointment to see Mary Welfsen. Tell her it's Don Robak."

The typist looked dubiously from the old lady to me, but she finally banged shut the glass and went back to her desk and used the intercom.

The old lady said, "I bet they won't give you nothing either, young man. They only gives it to them that bows and scrapes and kisses good at them." She sniffed. "Damned bastards."

Mary Welfsen came to a door and beckoned, rescuing me.

I followed behind her down a central hall. She seemed trimmer than when we'd dated. Then she'd been a slightly overweight girl, her features vaguely puffy, pretty, but pudgy.

In cubicle offices on either side of the hall employees worked on records, talked on telephones, or discussed things in groups. Most of the employees were women. One local wag had once told me that any man seen entering the welfare office after working hours would automatically be arrested for burglary.

"Who's the old lady out in the reception area?" I asked Mary Welfsen after she'd seated me in her cubicle. "And why are you refusing her food stamps?" I smiled to show I was on her side.

"A crazy. She's picketing us. She's old and she has plenty of money. She doesn't want to spend hers—she wants to spend ours." She smiled. "Not a bad idea at that."

"Thanks for seeing me."

"It suddenly has slackened up. I don't know why. Good weather maybe. Some times, many times even, there won't be an empty seat out there at this time of day." She smiled at me without either malice or liking, merely a curious smile. "What brings you here?"

"I'm representing a Miss Cheryl Rettner in her problems. I thought I could find out something over here, anything at all. About her, about the place she was staying, about the people who ran it and died. Anything at all."

"I don't know anything about the people she killed other than that they worked for us."

I held up a hand. "Please. At this stage she's merely *accused* of killing someone," I said without irritation. "I'm trying to understand things, how it went wrong for her out there."

She frowned and considered me. "I doubt there'd be anything for you in this office."

"Can I ask some questions?"

"Of me?"

"Yes, of you."

"I suppose so."

"Does the house out there belong to the welfare department?"

"Where the people were murdered?"

I nodded patiently.

She shook her head. "We only operate it, license it. The house belongs to a church. There are places around we do own, or at least I think there are. We just have a contract with that one."

"Is the owner Bishop Shooken's church?"

"I don't know. It isn't my department." She looked at me and then away. "It probably is his church, but don't say I said it until you check."

"Do you know Bishop Shooken?"

"Yes. I know most of our local ministers, even the far-out ones. He's not the most far-out, by the way. We do a lot of our business through and with the ministers. They usually know about people in need and in trouble before we do. And Bishop Shooken is in and out of here more than most of the others."

"Do you talk to him?"

"Not often. He talks mostly with the director, I think. Or maybe with one of the other case workers." She transfixed me with a direct stare. "Why?"

"No substantial reason. I'm exploring the edges of the case I've seen. I'm very interested in who owns the house where the killings took place. I'm interested in knowing as much as I can about not only the owners, but also the Davidsons when they were the operators of the house. Would it be possible for me to get a copy of whatever agreement the department has made on that house, if there is such a thing?"

"Not from me," she said.

"All right," I said agreeably. "Who do I see to get what I want?"

"I suppose either the director or the board, next time they have a meeting. The director is appointed by the board. The members of the board are named by various appointing authorities, circuit judge, county commissioners and council, mayor, city council. There are five on the board—I guess one named by each appointing authority." She nodded to herself, somehow pleased, I thought. "It's a thankless enough job—maybe they draw a hundred dollars a year."

"Who are the members of the board just now?"

"I hesitate to tell you because I know you have a suspicious mind, but I suppose if I don't tell you then someone else will."

I nodded, suddenly knowing what she was going to say. "You're going to tell me that Bishop Shooken's on the board?"

She nodded.

"And so he does a little business with himself when he rents his house or houses to the welfare department?"

"I suppose he'd probably abstain from the voting. Besides that the house in question is only leased and doesn't belong to him personally. It belongs to his church."

"You know more about it than I thought you did originally."

She blushed, but only a little. "There's a difference, you know."

"Is there now?" I asked. Maybe there was and maybe there wasn't. It seemed worth pursuing. "I'd sure like to see the contracts," I repeated.

"If you're representing Cheryl Rettner then can't you get what you need with a court order?"

"I can if I can show a court I need it to prepare for trial. My problem is that I don't know that until I have a look beforehand."

She shook her head slowly. "I'm not going to get into trouble digging my way into files where I have no business." She held up a hand as I started to reply. "How about if I tell you a place where you maybe could go and see a copy without any problems?"

"You'd be a sweetheart, Mary."

"Then try the auditor's office. Anytime we enter into a contract we furnish them a copy because they write the checks. Do you know the county auditor?"

I nodded. I not only knew him, we were sort of friends.

"Then try there."

"I will, Mary, with thanks. One more thing. I was at that house and I've talked with several of the kids who stay there. They tell me there isn't very much food. I wonder could you or someone, unknown to Bishop Shooken and the Allens, make a surprise stop out there at a mealtime or two?"

She hesitated. "I suppose I might stop myself. Kate's my case. She normally comes in here, but I could go out there."

"Kate James is your case?"

"Yes. I like her. She's so damned bright. She's learned

to absorb the world around her like a little sponge." She nodded. "I'll go past and surprise her."

"Do it when Shooken isn't there. You might check the condition of the house also. It looked pretty bad when I was out there."

"All right."

"Thanks, Mary."

I drew a careful, perhaps wistful look. "I've heard you were going to get married, Don."

"It's possible. Some days I hope so."

"And other days?"

I smiled at her. "No one is ever sure, Mary."

The auditor of my county is a man named William Dean Elrod, commonly known as "Wild Bill." He's getting old and he's dingy-looking. He wears tacky suits and narrow ties and chews almost constantly at a cud of tobacco. When the county commissioners were considering cute Treasurer Frieda's spittoons-into-flower-pots request he'd sat in on the meeting, chewing all the time and placing the by-product loudly into a spittoon he'd carried in from the hall. Needless to say the measure lost. Before he was auditor he was treasurer and before that he'd worked as an assistant. He was a friend I'd inherited. He'd been very close to Senator Adams, who'd been my partner until he died. I'd fallen heir to whatever good will there was left over from that relationship.

The auditor resembles a courthouse football quarterback. Everything passes through the auditor's office. Moneys spent must be okayed there, the checks drawn and countersigned. Tax books begin their complicated, transitory life there and all property sold is first of all transferred for tax purposes. New appropriations and additional expenditures begin and annual budgets of all office holders must be filed in the auditor's office. The auditor keeps the files of expenditures of the other county offices, takes their proposals before the commissioners and council as a sort of an ex-officio member of those boards.

Wild Bill was running a complicated-looking adding machine or calculator of some sort. His old liver-spotted hands moved with agility on the keys. Someone had informed me he was pushing eighty, but he seemed much younger. He completed his mathematics and looked up at me.

"There you is, Honest Don," he said affably enough. "What you want, boy?" He drummed on his desk. In the windows beside him he kept pictures of his direct descendants. Six children, each of whom had married and had children, some of whom were married and had children. There were about fifty pictures. What with in-laws it was no wonder he kept getting elected.

"I'd like to look over your contract file on the welfare department."

He clicked his tongue idly, a man with available time for any taxpayer even if that taxpayer was also a lawyer. Tolerant. "I heard you was the one for that pretty little girl over there. I seen them bringing her to court that first day. Do it have anything to do with that?"

I nodded.

"Well I wouldn't want to get out in the road and block equal justice for all," he said, smiling only a little, exposing worn plates. "You just wait right here and I'll see what I can dig up for you."

I went back to the counter and stood and waited. In the back of his office two girls worked their own machines and watched me curiously. I winked at the younger one, a girl probably no more than three or four years older than Cherry. She blushed prettily and looked back down at her machine.

Wild Bill brought out a fair-sized cardboard box and placed it on the counter.

"Maybe what you want would be in here. I keep most of the county contracts here. There ain't that many of them." He opened the box and began to thumb expertly through papers.

"Nope," he rebuked himself. "That stack's highway, dummy." He thumbed on. "Yep. Here they is." He drew out a medium-thick Manila folder and handed it to me.

"Don't you dare take none of these things outside my office," he warned severely and then winked broadly. "They's a copy machine you can use down in the recorder's office." He walked back to his machine and soon had it merrily blinking and spinning again.

I thumbed through the file. There were many papers. Most of them meant nothing to me. I finally came on a long, printed contract. It was complex, but after I'd explored it for a while, I found it was something about the use of federal funds.

At the bottom of the stack I found some rental contracts, half a dozen of them. Two of those contracts were close to identical and had been typed on the same typewriter. I set those two aside and glanced at the others first. Two of them were lease agreements on homes for the aged. If Shooken or his group/church were involved there I couldn't discern it. The final two contracts contained the names of people I knew who were staunch Methodists.

The contracts I'd set aside I now read word for word.

They were disappointments to me also. Neither of them bore the name of either Shooken or a church. The first was between a man and wife named Wilson and Catherine Koontz and had to do with the operation of a "halfway home for delinquent and dependent youths." The Koontzs were to be paid six hundred dollars per month for the operation of that home plus nine dollars a day for each resident child. The second contract was very similar. It was between the now deceased Davidsons and the county welfare. Here the sum was nine hundred dollars a month and the per diem the same.

I stood there and thought about it. Shooken's failure to use his name upset me, but only for a moment. I thought it might be far more effective for me to "discover" what was going on in the midst of a trial, particularly if I could get him to lie to me about it on the stand.

I decided not to make copies. Wild Bill ran a tight office. The originals weren't going to disappear. If I made a point of making copies now someone would see what I was doing and the word would spread. I carried the Manila folder to Wild Bill's desk and dropped it there.

"Forget I asked to see this for a while if it doesn't cost you anything."

He shrugged carefully. "Okay," he said. I thought when I left he'd go over everything in the folder with a magnifying glass and two computers, but that was all right.

I went back out into the central hall of the courthouse. The benches were full. Inside the main door I could see the now familiar bulk of the twin who watched me. I leaned against the wall, thinking about what I'd just looked at and what it could mean. Around me farmers gossiped and aging alcoholics combined grubby pennies for one more pint of wine.

It was my bet that Shooken had managed the preparation of the contracts I'd just seen, carefully keeping his own name and the name of his cult out of them. I made myself a further bet that somewhere Shooken kept his own fileful of contracts and that among those papers were those affecting the Koontzs and Davidsons. A devious man, a planner.

I was pleased with what I'd found. It wasn't up to me to dig out all. I had no interest, for example, in items of evidence which helped establish Cherry's guilt, although I wanted to know about them in order to combat them.

What I was seeking were things to muddy the waters, to dim the coming testimony which would show Cherry, bloody knife in hand, crouched in the same room with the often-punctured Davidsons. I wanted areas in which to ask questions which might confuse, embarrass, or, best of all, cause a witness to lie to me. I wanted evidence of other motives and other alibi lacks.

All I needed was a quart of doubt. I'd found a little. The problem for me was that I didn't and wouldn't know when I had a quart and so I must continue, seeking further.

I moved on to the frustration of an old drunk I vaguely knew who was moving to bum me for drinking money. I outdistanced him.

It was lunchtime. I went back to the office, but Jake wasn't there. I had a brace of quick hamburgers downtown, wolfing them and sprinting onward. The filling station which had promised my car was only a few blocks away so I walked there. The LTD was ready.

I paid Iron Mike, who runs the station along with his two sons. It's a twenty-four-hour place, the only one like it downtown.

"Someone used what I'd guess was a pick on your tires," he explained. "We got 'em plugged okay." He stood there wringing huge hands, a half smile on his face. A year back a customer who'd brought a rolling wreck in for Iron Mike to do normal maintenance on had thereafter sued him because it was still a wreck when he'd driven it out. I'd defended and won and he liked me all right.

"All four tires," I mused.

"Why'd someone do that to you, Don?"

"Juvenile problems, Mike. I imagine it can and will happen again, maybe next time worse. Could I work out a temporary deal with you?"

"What sort of deal?"

"Could you let me park it here at the station when I'm not using it? No one, not even if they showed a note or I confirmed it by phone, would be permitted to use it. I exclude you and your sons. You could use it or move it, but no one else, no matter what they'd say. If someone came for it and said they had permission, just call the police." I nodded. "Particularly if the person wanting it should be a young, weight-lifter-type boy or boys."

"Sure, Don. Okay to leave it here. I'll tell the help and my sons and it'll be just the way you say. Park it right over there." He pointed to a place. "Smack under the light. Anyone tries anything we'd surely see them."

"Thanks, Mike."

He punched me lightly on the arm. "Hey, that's okay, Don. We watch it all right for you."

CHAPTER X

The juvenile court may authorize mental or physical examinations and treatment after a child has been found to be delinquent or dependent.

I pulled the car over where Iron Mike had directed and decided just to leave it there. I hiked back downtown. Doc Buckner wasn't back from lunch, but his office nurse confided that he was expected momentarily. I told her I'd be back and walked back toward the courthouse, looking here, looking there. If I was still being watched I saw no sign of it.

I spied a man sitting on the courthouse wall, a man I knew well, and had a sudden inspiration. His name was Wade "Preacher" Smyth. He was a friend. Once, years back, we'd played golf together, but then he'd given up golf along with other things.

He was as close as I thought I could reasonably come to someone who'd be a resident expert on the rocks and shoals of the fringe religions of Bington. Because of the university, cults had always flourished, but most of the ones I knew about were campus-based and died away when school was not in full session. Here it was, almost summer, and Shooken seemed prosperous.

One of Preacher's acquaintances had said that Preacher

was like a reluctant prostitute in his relationship with each new group he joined. He'd be saved just as she'd be raped. Let an itinerant arrive in Bington clad in robes and carrying a sign concerning the ending of the world, let a new cult gather, or a new man appear in one of the fringe churches, and Preacher would always be in the front row, eyes fierce, ready to chant or sing.

It wasn't a failing, it was the way he was. Someplace, years back now, he'd lost faith, took up drink, but was willing to trade the drink for a faith renewal any time one would happen.

He was a small, sixtyish man. His face seemed carved mostly out of large, yellow teeth. No matter what the weather he was always dressed in a funereal black suit. If he was going formal he wore a tie with it, usually also black. Today he was tieless.

When I'd first met him he'd been in real estate and he'd been very good at it. Now he did nothing. He'd had three wives. He'd quit working when the first one had died. The second one had been much younger than he was and had cleaned him out. The third one had some money of her own and he'd told me confidentially he had no intention of moving on from her.

Like most of the chronic wall sitters, he drank. His bouts were sudden and fierce. When he drank he went through a personality change and became more effusive and friendly than when sober. Sometimes, when a nondrinking period came along, he'd eschew the courthouse wall. Instead he'd stand across the street in the shadows and intently watch his former comrades. Should one of them cross the line into open drunkenness, fall down, fight, or sleep, Preacher would rush back to the sheriff's office, make his report and complaint, then watch righteously while deputies arrested the malefactor.

He'd been many times himself in the county jail and three hideous times to the state hospital for the sixty-day drying-out school.

He was a respected citizen of the wall, so respected that he was forgiven even the heinous sins he committed when he turned on his former friends during his fits of sobriety. He was asked for advice and often gave counsel to those with problems who requested it. Sometimes the advice he dispensed required consultation with a free lawyer. So I was valuable to him.

I beckoned him from his seat on the wall. Others watched apathetically or curiously, according to their state. I looked around again, trying to see if I was still under watch. If I was I saw nothing.

Preacher sidled close. I seldom began our encounters these days and I could see he was curious.

"You know a Bishop Shooken?" I asked.

He nodded. "I know him, Don." He nodded again, sizing me up. Some inner instinct made him realize I wanted dirt and not compliments. His breath smelled of sour wine as he talked. "He ain't so damn much. He's big and he can shout pretty good, but he don't talk from the Bible. He talks from hate, too much taxes, too much crime, too many people nosing after citizens. Bishop, my butt." He drew a little closer. "You know Miss Amy Bender?"

I nodded. I knew her. A righteous old lady who always carried an umbrella.

"She come to see you?"

"No."

"Well, I told her to see you. Her husband died, God rest him. She got going to Shooken's place, big, drafty-like barn out in the north county. Pretty soon he'd sweet-talked her out of all her money and her home place plus that rental she had up on Seventh Street. I don't know how he done it because Amy was always terrible tight with a penny, but he got it done and now she's going to sue him and his church."

"I see."

"He buys houses and turns them on conditional sale, Don. Miss you a payment and he'll show up with big guys and you're back in the street if he can do better with the house. He's got a bunch of bully boys who move you out."

"Great big boys? Young?"

"I guess."

"Weight-lifter types?" I persisted.

"I guess that's them. They do some stealing for him, too. Shooken sold a farmer I know named Cal Thacker about a hundred-plus acres and all the equipment in the farm barn on a walk-out sale. I seen the contract. Every night after that a piece of equipment would wander away, at first little stuff, then the big. It'd happen while Cal and his folks was at Shooken's meetings. Cal got suspicious of Shooken and lined up some friends and some shotguns and they found the equipment in a field back of the church and hauled it all back. I hear Cal had to quit going to meetings and disable or lock that stuff up every night from then on just to keep it. I also heard that Shooken got mad when Cal took the stuff back, claimed it wasn't the same pieces, and excommunicated Cal and his family." He looked up at me and smiled. "Cal had him a bad fire out there in his barn this spring. Shame about that. Maybe that's because Shooken kicked him out of his group. But Shooken's got a lot of others, Don. He visits them special, gives them things, acts like a good friend, then steals their shoelaces." He cackled approvingly.

"He owns the welfare house where them people named Davidson got killed," I confided.

Preacher nodded, digesting that tidbit. "And you got that girl they claim done it to defend. Is that it?"

"I'll be defending her."

"He likes girls, Shooken does. He's a big woman's man, pants after them hard. There's lots of stories about him and women." He smiled. "Sometimes, late at night when I can't sleep, I wish I was big like him and had back all my guile and loudness. I'd go back into real estate, make me a quick million, marry me a young one, then drink all the money up in fine wines, hundred dollars a bottle."

"You need money now?"

"I always need money. This wife keeps me on a short tether, she does." He looked toward the wall where sharp eyes appraised us. "I swear, that woman. But I'll need your money worse later. You keep it for me now. Pass anything here and it becomes community property. I'm in enough splits and deals to keep me wet for the rest of the day. And I've been thinking hard about quitting, maybe this time for good, Don. I've done it before. Once I stayed off for a whole year. The problem with me is when I get sober I see my world's been stolen away and all I've gotten is older."

Doc Buckner was in his office when I went back.

I entered and waited for a time and finally gained an audience. He took me to the room where he keeps all his diplomas and his medals from the K-War. He saved the room for when he had bad news for a patient. He'd told me that once. Today he'd evidently forgotten I knew.

"She said you were over to see her," I began.

He nodded. "She does have epilepsy. From her history which she gave me I'd say those seizures she has are now and have been psychomotor, maybe *grand mal*. I'd like to witness one and run some more tests before I commit myself, but she apparently has sensory and emotional aura, her consciousness becomes very clouded, perhaps occasional visual hallucinations. From what she told me I'd be willing to testify she could have had such an attack the night the Davidsons were killed."

I was a little encouraged. "I suppose the big question would be whether or not, while she was in such a seizure, could she have killed the Davidsons without intending to?"

"I'd have to answer that in my opinion she couldn't." He held up a hand to stop my questions. "I called a man in Chicago whom I know. He's a very good man and I'll give you his name if you want it. I put that question to him. He also said no. I doubt you'll find anyone who'll say substantially otherwise."

"How long could such a seizure put her under?"

"Most of them last only minutes, but some last longer. Sometimes a person can have one seizure following another. If it continues it can be life-threatening."

"But you're telling me she's lying when she says she doesn't remember what took place that night?"

"I'm not saying exactly that. From her past history, she does black out. But the acts that occurred while she says she was out would have required purpose on her part.

She'd have had to move from one victim to the next, wield the knife, cut and then slash. That doesn't fit with the claimed blackout."

"You're telling me then that she'd have had to be cognizant of the killings?"

"In my opinion, yes. There's one more thing you might do. Get her examined by a psychiatrist. With her background, with the fact that those people out there had abused her many times, plus the fact that the coming on of the attacks terrified her, she might have become hysterical prior to the blackout and done the misdeed then." He waved a hand. "Not my field."

"You don't believe it though, do you?"

He smiled. "Not a bit of it. She remembers, Don. She'll tell you she thinks she killed them. Wait long enough and she'll also tell you she remembers part or all of it. She's just conveniently forgotten the act for now. It's a defense mechanism." He looked away and then back. "Even now, when she's trying hard, she doesn't tell a very convincing story. I wasn't convinced. I doubt a jury will be impressed."

A last chance sort of idea occurred to me. "She belongs to a peculiar cult. I've never seen its meetings in operation, but I've heard stories. The minister of the cult may have fooled with her, fondled her, or more. She was forced to attend the services. The minister came around when she had seizures and tried to exorcise them. Could anything like that contribute to her situation and condition now?"

"You don't give up, do you?" He shook his head. "I can't think of anything which will get you where you want to go."

"This cult is all thunderation and hell-raising and loud music and lots of excitement." I thought a moment longer. It seemed worth enough to ask, "Would you go with me and take a look? That way I might be able to ask you questions at the trial of a hypothetical nature, adding what you see in as an additional fact."

"I don't know. I'm pretty busy, Don."

"I think maybe the minister, during his exorcism, got very enthusiastic."

"You said he tampered with her, but she didn't tell me that."

"Would you go?"

"Okay," he said, still not keen about it.

"There's supposed to be music," I added.

Buckner was a music nut. "That would be some reason to go even if yours is not," he said, sighing a little. "Sorry I can't be of more help."

I went back to my office and moped around. Jake was in a hearing, but had left word with the secretaries that he wanted to see me.

I moved from my office to his after a while and sat on his couch and dug into the stack of advance sheets I was behind on. After a long time I ran onto the case where hypnotism was involved. A woman had been involved in a bad auto accident. She'd been unable to remember the accident or events before or afterward. When hypnotized she'd remembered. She'd been deposed, that is her testimony had been taken down under oath, prior to the time she was hypnotized. A judge had allowed the new testimony into evidence over the objections of the other side for "what it was worth." Opposing counsel had vigorously cross-examined her. The appellate court had upheld the ruling of the court mostly on the ground that a judge had wide latitude in what was admissible and what was not. The case was civil, but it ought to be precedent in a criminal case also. I set the case aside thoughtfully for further study.

I had a moment of sudden, clear realization. Cherry hadn't been interested in being hypnotized. I knew I wasn't going to get her to change her mind. Maybe she didn't want to remember what had happened or, more likely, she already remembered.

I still had to defend her. I'd taken her on as a client and now, while I remained her lawyer, it was my job to help her. Belief, as a concept, is a vague thing in law. A jury believes what a jury sees and hears, not what actually occurred. Some things never make it into evidence, other things are forgotten or ignored.

Jake returned about closing time.

"Catching up at last," he said, pleased at all the advance sheets stacked around me.

I nodded.

"I served the deposition notices on the prosecutor late yesterday. I got a call from the prosecutor today. He told me those boys aren't going to answer questions without having their own lawyer present and he thought the same thing would apply to the other witnesses we wanted to depose other than the sheriff. The boys have a lawyer. Luke Taplinger called me and said he'd be representing them and others. He said the boys told him that you were after them and had said you were going to try to make them look guilty instead of your client." He nodded at me, dead serious. "Taplinger wants to meet with you before any depositions are attempted. He said if you weren't willing he was going to try to get an order from Steinmetz to do what you want by interrogatories."

"I'm entitled to depose witnesses."

"Sure. But with Luke there they just aren't going to answer any questions they don't like or Luke doesn't like and that'll be most of them."

"That's not the way it works."

"Well, it's the way Luke does it. He just tells his people not to answer until ordered by a court. He's peculiar. You know that. Herman Leaks sounded pleased about it on the phone."

"He would be," I said. "How about Bishop Shooken and those people who run the house now?"

"Well, as I said, the revolution's spread. Luke now represents them also." He shook his head dolefully. "Another thing of interest. When I was sniffing around over at the courthouse one of the girls in the clerk's office said that one of the boys came in over there recently and asked to see the court rules. She said he glanced through them quickly and gave them back. She told me he was a big boy with reddish hair."

"Angler," I said. "He's probably memorized the rules and now he'll spit them back at us one by one."

"What do you want to do about the depositions? I set them all for late next week."

"Leave them on. If Luke tries to stop them we can ask for a hearing. All this gives me the urge to file a motion for a speedy trial and force Herman's hand. Maybe if I don't get to depose his witnesses there's a chance the judge won't let him call them in the trial."

Jake shook his head. "All he'd do is grant you a continuance to take your depositions. And he'd be right."

"I suppose."

CHAPTER XI

The right to full freedom of worship in this state shall not be abridged.

I picked up Doc Buckner after obtaining the LTD at Iron Mike's station. No one had been around to bother the vehicle, according to Iron Mike's oldest son, who was running things when I went past.

We rode north into the twilight. I pushed at Doc again. "How about drugs? Could they affect her?"

He nodded over at me. "What you really want me to say isn't possible. Even if I fell all the way over backwards and let you seduce me on the stand I still would never be able to say she could be blacked out and still retain the ability to wield the knife the way she obviously did. Sheriff Abraham flashed me his grisly pictures after I'd been in to see her. I looked them over, but I said nothing to him or to anyone else." He smiled again. "After all I'd just received a dollar for my services from your client and my patient."

"All I'm trying to do is understand," I said. "You doctors control such mysteries and we poor lawyers have only our thirst for knowledge."

He grinned at me.

"What would the effects be, if prior to her attack or spell, she'd been given some kind of drug?"

"What kind of drug?"

"Angel dust," I said. I'd heard there was a lot of that around. "Cocaine. Hashish. You tell me what drug could cause problems and I'll try to dig it up for you."

He shook his head. "I'm just not that much of an expert. I think you need to do your shopping soon for a good, trial-type psychiatrist, a man of strong beliefs and with an easy courtroom manner. Not some poor, broken-down G.P. Maybe if you'd lay your stuff on him just right and up front you might get him to go your way. I've never heard of it happening the way you want me to say it could have happened."

"But no one else knows you feel this way?"

"No. Not from me. Another doctor, if asked, might tell the opposition exactly what I'm telling you."

"Another doctor isn't going to get to check her. At least not yet. If the prosecutor thinks or I can make him think I've got something it's almost as good as having something."

"Doesn't it make you feel peculiar when you tamper in things like this, attempt to make them come out the way you want?"

"Not at all," I said. "I'm not being creative. I'm only working with what's available."

"Well, I won't say a solitary thing except on your command, mighty master."

I nodded and concentrated on keeping the LTD on the narrow asphalt, no easy task. I followed the directions I'd read in the Bington *Chronicle* to the "church."

In a while, after rushing through the warm evening, we found it.

The building was huge and old. Perhaps it had once been a church, perhaps a lodge, but it seemed to me that

I recalled it as abandoned for a long time. Now the weeds had been mowed, the broken windows repaired or covered over with boards, and the building freshly painted. The rutted, gravel parking lot was crowded with vehicles, most of them either pickup trucks or dilapidated old farm cars. One small light hung from a pole near the church to illuminate the walk and the nearest part of the parking lot. I carefully picked my spot to park. I found one where it wasn't far out to the road and where I could gain access to that road without turning around.

There were bumper stickers on some of the trucks and cars. They read, "God Is Alive and Satan Defeated."

A new sign, freshly painted also, had been erected by the walk. "Satan Defeated Group," it announced boldly. The name must have been newly adopted, because I'd not seen it in any ads.

No one seemed to be watching from outside. On a hunch, I hopped up on the wall by the steps and unscrewed the light bulb and put it in my pocket while Doc Buckner watched reprovingly.

From inside we could hear the sound of a trumpet, sweet and clear. Doc Buckner punched me heavily on the arm in the darkness.

"Hear? Hear? That's my kind of music."

I felt eyes on us as we went in the double doors. The back of the church was crowded with men in overalls and women in cheap dresses. I smelled bay rum mixed with strong perfume, all of it overlaid with perspiration. I could spot no seats downstairs, but steps led upward and so we creaked up them to what seemed more like a loft than a balcony. There were a few folding-chair seats left there.

The front of the building was lit by tiers of candles.

There was a raised center podium. Bishop Shooken stood there, dressed imposingly in white satin. He was flanked on both sides by men in shiny black suits with black string ties. Behind them a young trumpet player, no more than twenty or so, played with only an uncertain and unseen organ to accompany him. He was also dressed in black. He was playing a song I thought I remembered, a spiritual, and playing it very well. He played in clear notes, at his own pace, in his own style. I could see his eyes follow Shooken worshipfully.

"Put that boy with a base and a piano and he could draw a crowd in any bar in Bington," Doc whispered loudly.

People were watching.

"Shhhh," I whispered. At one corner of the loft I spied a sharp-eyed man, dressed in the black suit of authority. He was observing us carefully. He must have made up his mind, for soon he slipped through the loft crowd and down the stairs.

When I'd confronted Shooken at the welfare house and later at the bar he'd seemed merely ponderous. The stories I'd heard and my encounters with him had made him a slightly ridiculous figure in my eyes. He was someone only to be looked quickly over, lightly examined, a thief of a differing nature, but still a thief.

Inside his "church" he was different.

He exuded power. He raised his eyes and brought immediate silence. I rapid-counted the house and estimated that, upstairs and down, there might be as many as three or four hundred people, waiting and watching Shooken just as I was doing.

His voice was deep and good. "I am here and you are

here to do the work, perform the orders, and carry out the Commandments. All this no matter how much those of evil power would try to obstruct and defeat us." He looked around his room and his eyes caught light from the candles. "Even if we must die for it.

"Satan is defeated in our souls, but the world remains filled with his devout followers, with those who traded their souls for the powers he gave them. I mean those who sit as lawyers and prosecutors and judges. The ones we must hate and destroy. Their laws are not for us, my followers."

I looked around and saw that he owned the crowd.

Doc Buckner moved restlessly beside me. "What is this?" he whispered.

Someone rumbled harshly in the darkness of the loft, "Shut up over there."

Shooken: "The time draws nigh to the day I will direct you to take back all power to ourselves, to punish them, to return the law to the ten laws which must be followed, but exclude from their protection the followers of Satan. That time, that day, will be on us soon."

At a corner of the podium I saw the note passed. It went from hand to hand and finally reached Shooken. He took it and frowned at the interruption and made a tiny gesture which brought the ready trumpet up shrilly in what sounded almost like a call to arms.

Shooken read the note and I saw the veins in his neck swell. He crumpled the note into a tiny ball and dropped it before him. At the same time his eyes came up to the balcony and sought me, but I stayed low. The trumpet player did a run of high notes.

"Listen to that," Doc whispered unaware, entranced again at the music.

"I think it's past time for us to be on our way," I said.

"Wait now," Buckner commanded, still listening hard, frowning at my statement.

Another gesture from Bishop Shooken and all sound stopped.

"Some of those men of power who hate and defraud us are among us tonight, spying on us," Shooken said. "I'm told that defenders of the murder of two of our staunch group are here to smell and pry and scoff." He leaned forward and I was afraid. "I say to you now and I say to them that the time for following our laws is now. Our words mean all, while their obscene courthouse gesturings mean nothing. Look around you, my followers. You will discover them."

People were looking and craning. Down below a commotion broke out as someone found a stranger. The light in the loft was dim. It was a long time past safe departure. I pulled hastily at Doc and he came willingly enough now. We scrambled to the steps. Hands reached out, but I brushed them aside and kept going down. Once down, the way again seemed blocked, but someone recognized Doc.

"That's only Doc Buck," a voice commanded in the crowd. "He's a good old boy. Let him through."

We threaded our way to the door. No further hand was raised.

"All right," Shooken called regretfully, seeing us go. "Let them run for now. Let them retreat into their darkness. This time let them escape, but only this time." The trumpet swelled again.

Outside a pair of black-clads waited ominously, but the night was very dark and the bulb to the light remained in my pocket.

"Behind us," I called. "Bishop Shooken said to tell you to hold them for him."

It didn't confuse them much. One of them called us a name and swung strongly at me, but he was slow and I ducked the punch and was around him quickly and into the depths of the parking lot, Doc close behind me. There was yelling from the church.

"What's this all about?" Doc called in bewilderment, running as fast as I was.

I got us into the LTD and out of the lot and onto the asphalt road. Behind I could see some minor scurrying here and there, but there seemed not to be any immediate purposeful pursuit.

"Boy," Doc said, breathing hard.

"Silence," I ordered.

He looked over at me with a perplexed expression. "Jesus, Don. I don't know about that place. He seemed like he could do anything with those people."

"Cheryl Rettner was forced to attend there. How about your testimony now?"

"I don't know about that, but tell me what that was all about."

"You're a man of power, a follower of Satan. You read dirty, watch dirty, talk dirty, drink and smoke dirty."

He looked at me, mildly upset by what I was saying. Suddenly something which had not been funny, but ugly, changed so that we whooped and roared and infected each other with more whoops and roars.

I had to slow down as we beat each other on the back.

I drove him to his office and there he invited me inside and gave me two stiff drinks of Early Times.

In the morning I ran. I got up, put on my running shoes and a light sweat suit. I made the mistake of taking my normal route, down from the apartment to the river, then upriver for what was to be two-plus miles.

They lay in wait for me and got me when I came over the last hill to the path. They'd picked a very good, deserted spot. There were three of them, Angler and the twins. One of them must have been behind me, tracking me, someplace where I'd not spotted him.

With a fifty-yard head start I could probably have outrun them, worn them out, then pulled away. But Angler had undoubtedly planned on that. He blocked the path. One of the twins had cut me off forward. I turned and the second twin came up over the hill behind me. He smiled wolfishly.

"Come to papa," Angler called. "Come on, small man. Angler needs to tell you something in the only way Angler feels you'll understand and remember."

I decided Angler might be quicker than either of the bulky twins and so I stayed toward the twin coming down the hill, intending to evade capture, and moved back up on the road instead of staying trapped on the path below.

I almost made it. I got under a huge arm, but the second twin kicked one of my legs out from under me and I teetered near the top and fell back. I yelled out, thinking I saw a flash of color coming from far away.

The twins sat on me, one high and one low. Angler drew close.

"You keep messing around where you oughtn't, Mr. Lawyer. I told you all you needed to do was to go in and do your lawyer stuff and let us handle things, but you don't do that." He smiled down at me, but his face was red. "I warned you. We been watching. You keep diddling around and messing up things, embarrassing Bishop Shooken, saying things to him. You've got to stop that."

"I'm trying to do what I was hired to do."

"You even decided on those depositions after what I told you. Now we're maybe going to have to turn on Cherry. We're going to say things you'll not get around, Mr. Robak. You're not going to get her off by making us look guilty. Murder's the one crime that they can hold us on without bond. So you try Cherry, not us, nor Bishop Shooken, nor anyone else."

"What's Shooken mean to you, Angler? Why'd you let him mess with your girl?" I tried to push out of the holds I was in, wriggling hard, but it was like trying to move mountains. The twins were very strong.

"The good bishop gets us out of jail, man. He talks for us. Once or twice we've been waived into adult court in other counties and he gets up our bond. If someone has to sign for something then he signs. He's all right with us. We help him, he helps us. It could be that way with you, too."

"Angler, I know you're on parole. I could complain and back you'd go."

He smiled. "Complain away, Mr. Robak. They don't want me up there and I got my parole officer snowed. He thinks I'm the brightest around. He won't send me back. So you'd better do like I tell you."

"I have to do things my way," I said.

He lost patience. "Then do them hurting." He kicked me in the ribs, driving the wind from me, making me go sick and cold. The twin at my face smiled down at me, enjoying my pain.

"You say you know about waivers?" I asked.

"We know about them, Mr. Robak. We've been waived in other areas, but not here. The prosecutor here has never asked for one. And even if you could get us waived to adult court the bishop would bond us out. So quit threatening us. We're running this show, not you."

The twin by my face raised a huge, threatening hand.

"Don't mark him," Angler ordered that twin. "Don't hit him in the face." He moved around to my other side and kicked me again very hard, getting me just below the rib cage.

I pushed and heaved weakly and without results. The twins stayed solidly in place.

"Too many kicks can kill you, Mr. Robak. You want to die to prove your point?" He looked down at me and smiled. "We've heard around you was a hardhead."

Up on the bank I spied movement. Someone called, "Hey! Hey!"

"Remember now," Angler said to me in a low voice. He gestured to the twins and they rolled off, laughing.

"Just a game," Angler called up to the watchers on the bank above. "Just playing."

I struggled to get up, but was momentarily unable to make it. Angler smiled fondly down at me.

"You're not as tough as you thought, Mr. Robak. Maybe we'll meet again if you don't do it our way. Remember now. No hard feelings, but you'd best stop fooling around. Leave Bishop Shooken alone. Leave us alone."

Up above on the bank two older men in heavy sweat suits, joggers I'd seen occasionally before, stood watching us with interest. I got them in focus and managed to laboriously stand.

By the time I could do that the boys were a hundred yards away, running swiftly, laughing among themselves.

"Thanks for stopping," I called up to the two men. They nodded and moved on, not wanting to inquire into my troubles now that they seemed momentarily over.

I walked around a little. I was very sore, but I felt I could run. Angler and the twins had vanished. I ran my course up the river and then back, working hard, hurting some. I was still very sore when the run was over, but a shower helped.

When I got out of the shower someone was banging on my front door. I put on an old robe and opened up. It was Gates Taine, my reporter friend.

"I thought maybe the only way to catch you was to come past. I keep calling your office, but you're either not there or they say you're not there. I had something I wanted to show you."

"Come inside, Gates. Want some coffee? I was just going to fix some."

He nodded and followed me back to my small kitchen. I put on water, dished instant coffee into cups, and waited for the water to come to a boil.

Gates handed me a folded paper.

"The advertising manager gave me this," he said. "You're mentioned."

It was an advertisement for Bishop Shooken's ongoing "revival" for law and order. It was pretty much the same as what I'd already seen except that in the right-hand corner there was a list of public enemies. My name was there. So was Cheryl Rettner's, plus that of the chief justice of our state court, Judge Steinmetz's, a couple of federal judges, and a lot of names I didn't recognize.

"Most of these people I don't know," I said, pointing at the names.

He smiled. "I wasn't for sure who all of them were at first, but one name rang a bell. There's some wanted criminals on the list. He must have gotten those names off the posters at the sheriff's office or in the post office. But what's he got you and Steinmetz and those others there for?" He held up a hand to stop me. "We refused to run it of course and he got very incensed. He said he was going to get it printed up as handbills and add our name to the list. Is he crazy?"

"That's a good guess," I said. I described what I'd seen and heard the night before. Halfway through my narrative he started taking notes.

"We got a new guy we can send out there," he said, when I was done. "Fresh in town. Oh boy, oh boy, what a whacko. I'm going to smack him good, Don." He nodded to himself and gave me a thoughtful look. "He really said all that stuff?"

"He really did. If you want to check on it Doc Buckner was with me. Get someone to dig around on Shooken's welfare situation, too. That could be the very best part."

He shook his head. "That's a follow-up story, not the first shot." He eyed me, still without complete belief. "He owns those places where they keep the kids? Including the place where the Davidsons died?"

"One way or another he owns them. He runs the show and collects the money. You dig out how."

He sipped his coffee. "He hates you more than the others. The advertising manager said he offered to compromise on his ad and drop Judge Steinmetz and some others, but he wouldn't drop you. Why is that, Don?"

I smiled and rubbed my injured ribs gently. I'd not told him about that.

I said, "Because I'm evil, Gates."

He shook his head wisely. "No. He hates you because you're like him, just as he's like you. You don't look alike— that isn't it. But I happen to know that he was once a lawyer. Now he hates the law and lawyers and judges. You're still a lawyer. I think he sees in you what he might have been." He looked away and then back. "And maybe you see in him what you might become."

"That's very deep," I said, not liking it much.

He smirked at me.

After Gates left I lolled around for a while and watched kiddie television, Saturday-morning stuff, selling toys, selling dreams. The pain in my side and back slowly subsided. About eleven o'clock the phone rang. It was Doc Buckner calling from the local hospital.

"There's a man in over here who wants to talk with you. He asked me to call."

"Is he a bishop or only an acolyte?" I asked, thinking he was kidding.

"Neither one. His name is Alvin Lucas Endsley and he got stomped pretty good in a downtown alley last night. Someone laid for him and broke both his hands. He said you'd know him as Cyclops."

"Thanks, Doc," I said, distressed. "You tell him I'll be right over."

I walked to the filling station and got my car. I had no

apparent watcher. I drove to the hospital, watching behind. No one.

At the reception desk a volunteer told what room Cyclops was in and how to get there. I rode up an elevator that shimmied in its shaft and smelled like flowers mixed with ether.

They had him propped up in bed. He didn't look too good. Both eyes were black and his face was scratched and swollen. His right hand and lower arm were covered by a large cast. His left arm and hand were even worse, out at an angle from his body in one of those special lift casts doctors construct.

He was awake. He gave me a sad, small smile.

"I just wanted you to know I was here," he said apologetically. "You didn't have to come. There already have been lots of police around, but I didn't help them much." He shook his head. "Nothing to tell."

"Who did it, Cyclops?"

"I ain't for sure." He looked away from me at his antiseptically white wall. "Truly. I mean truly, I ain't sure. I went to the alley back of Eddo's place and someone got me one on the head. I got a call to meet someone there. I didn't know who it was that called. I guess maybe I should have found out before I went." He nodded. "It could have been someone I beat bad playing pea pool or eight ball. I don't know."

"Sure," I said, knowing who he was leaving out. "Did you see or hear anything at all?"

"I heard a little. After they dropped me I can remember laying there and hearing someone say something about getting my hands. I was bad fogged, but I remember that. And I think there was more than one doing it."

"Did you do any questioning around on my thing, Cyclops?"

He shook his head righteously. "Not me. You said not. I just listened. I told a couple of guys I know to listen also, but that wasn't like asking questions, was it, Don?" He thought for a minute. "When I got the call to go back to the alley I thought maybe it was one of those guys calling."

I sighed. "That's all right, Cyclops. And you did fine, just right. Now I want you to forget completely about Cherry and her problems and just work on getting well."

"Okay."

"I want to ask one more thing. You said once that you found the knife you loaned Cherry. You wouldn't have maybe borrowed that knife from someone?"

"You mean stolen it? I never. I swear, Don."

I believed him.

He looked away again. "I heard a nurse say that maybe my hands . . ."

"I talked with Doc Buckner," I said. "I'll bet they'll be fine. I'll bet you on that."

He nodded hopefully. I sat beside his bed and, in a while, he dropped off to sleep. I searched for and found Buckner down in the emergency room.

"How bad is he?" I asked, when he had a moment.

"Hard to tell. Someone stomped him up pretty good, particularly his hands. A mean job. He may or may not have some permanent disability."

I moved restlessly, nervous to be around a hospital, glad I was a lawyer and not a doctor. My rib pain had come back a little.

"Watch yourself, Doc. Stay out of dark, deserted places. Be careful of calls you don't understand. I don't think you'll be bothered, but you were with me last night and I'm not liked in certain circles."

He nodded perfunctorily without real comprehension.

"Thanks for calling," I said. "If Cyclops needs money help I'm available." I shook my head. "Whoever it was knew enough to ruin his one joy."

I went back to the apartment and put on knit pants and an old, soft hound's-tooth jacket. I started making the rounds of the bars in Bington, concentrating on those I knew had music.

I found Martha Angler in the third place I visited, Chop's Place, a piano bar sort of joint.

I'd been expecting something else, something dried up and diseased because of the story Judge Steinmetz had told me.

She wasn't like that at all.

I'd been in Chop's before. They kept the piano going most of the time, making up in quantity what was lacking in quality. I got a drink and asked the bartender, whose face I vaguely knew, if he knew a lady named Angler.

He pointed to the piano bar. A woman sat in the closest seat to the piano player, urging him on.

"That's Martha."

I moved over that way. There wasn't an available seat close to her although there were some on the other side. Instead of going over there I stood behind her and watched her. In a little while she felt my eyes on her and turned and smiled directly at me. I gave her a small toast with my glass.

She was quite handsome. Her hair was red, so obviously dyed that it didn't offend. She'd curled it into tiny ringlets. Her body was very good. She was a big woman, perhaps close to six feet, but everything about her was big and fit with the rest. When she smiled at me her eyes were both calculating and interested.

In a bit the seat next to her opened and I took it. She looked me over again.

"You're new," she said. "I've never seen you around here before."

"I was looking for you," I said, smiling.

She took it as a compliment instead of the truth and nodded her head coquettishly.

"I sing here," she explained to me. "After while I'll sing for you."

"I'd like that. After another while can I buy you a drink or three?"

"Sure now," she said enthusiastically. "Sure you can, honey."

There was a small, hand microphone on the piano. The supercilious piano player, who wasn't that great, handed it to her tolerantly and she sang. She wasn't bad, not bad at all. She had very good timing. She sang "Release Me," and then a song about a big, black whale I'd never heard before, full of double meanings, very cutesy, but made for someone with good timing.

An hour later we were old friends. I'd bought her several J & B scotches and had nipped sparingly myself at a bit of Early Times. We were in a booth in the back of the room. The piano player was taking a break and it was dark in the booth. She had one leg planted firmly against mine.

"You say you're a lawyer?" she asked. Her voice was only slightly thick.

I nodded.

"Seems to me like I just read your name in the local paper yesterday."

There had been a story about me representing Cheryl Rettner in recently.

"I'm representing a young girl who's accused of killing two people."

Her eyes went a little blank, but the constant pressure of leg on leg didn't slacken. It was a pleasant enough sensation.

I snapped my fingers. "Hey, Martha, one of the kids out there at the place where it happened has the same name as yours—Angler."

Pressure lessened momentarily. "My name ain't Angler. It's Smith. Martha Smith."

I shook my head positively. "I liked what I saw and asked before I came over. I got told your name was Martha Angler."

She drank her drink dry and nodded gloomily. I gave the sign to a nearby waitress for another drink for her.

"Probably my kid. Rotten kid." She smiled. "Used to call him 'Junior' and he'd go red-dog mad. Crazy kid. Always in trouble. I saw him on the street not too long ago, but he wouldn't even talk to me." She shook her head. "I don't care at all."

"Sure you do," I said soothingly. "I talked with him out there. He's a real bright boy, very smart."

"His father was smart. He could do figures in his head. Didn't have to write numbers down. He got killed working. I could have got some money for that, but we'd already busted up." Her leg moved back against mine. "Let's get out of here?"

"I thought you had to sing?"

"Not now, Don. Not anytime unless I want. The piano doesn't start up again until six." She glanced at her wristwatch. "That's more than an hour. Sometimes, if something happens, I don't come back." She gave me a smile. Her eyes calculated me for value, an asking price.

"Another drink and then onward?" I asked.

"Sure. Okay."

"He's sure a big kid," I mused, to get her started again.

"His father was a big man. I'm big. He comes by size natural enough. I did the best I could for him, but he was a sure enough problem child. He was a sweet baby, but he had to have his own way when he got older. I took him to see a child psychologist one time. He got real interested in him and wanted me to bring him back. He told me to be careful."

"Because he was so smart, you mean?"

"No, not that. Not that at all." She reached out with a big, well-formed hand and took mine warmly. I thought she was at least a semipro, but she was still tempting. "He said he had some kind of mind trouble. Not bad, but it could be. Didn't care about anyone else. Always figuring how to make it come out his way. He could lie right in your face even then." She shook her head. "His daddy shouldn't have run off and left us."

"How did your son wind up at that place where the people were killed?"

"Kept getting in more and more trouble." She shivered. "When he was about eleven I think he tried to kill me. I never was sure, but it scared me bad. Some damage got done to my car brakes, things the garage told me about, but I didn't understand. I had a wreck because of it.

Later I found some car-repair books he'd hidden away under his bed. When I could ditch him I ditched him and I'm not sorry. Cold little man. Hated me. Hated the name Junior." She lifted her glass and inspected it for flaws.

It seemed to me, watching her, that life had damaged her just as it had her son. The areas of loss were different, but the damage was there in both of them. I was sorry for them, but Cherry was my client. I found myself wondering, if Angler testified and hurt Cherry, could I use his mother to impeach his testimony? *Cold little man. Tried to kill me.*

I thought I could.

We didn't manage to leave. I bought her another drink and then others. At six o'clock the piano player returned, saw she was still there, and waved her over. My leg felt warm where hers had pressed it.

She sang "September Song" to me. After that I escaped by going to the men's room and then on down the hall and out a back door.

CHAPTER XII

Any person convicted of entering a place of human habitation with the intent to commit a felony therein shall be punished by . . .

While the sun was still up I drove out the road that paralleled the river to near the welfare house. To the best of my ability to watch no one followed. I thought maybe they now figured I no longer needed watching. After all, they'd given me and my acquaintance, Cyclops, our lessons in what happened to those who trespassed in Angler's life.

I parked behind the copse of trees where I'd once picked up Kate James, hiding the car so that it couldn't be seen from the road. There was still some light and so I walked through the trees, taking care to stay out of sight. I found a vantage point and watched the welfare house. There was activity there. I could see someone moving around inside and, after a while, Kate came out onto the porch with a book and sat down to read. After another while the light grew dim enough to discourage her and she went back inside.

On my way back to the car I saw what looked like a tended patch of ground back of the trees, cunningly hidden. I walked to it. Someone had dug up a patch of ground maybe ten feet by twenty feet. Green shoots grew from the ground in orderly, planted rows. I didn't know what marijuana looked like under cultivation, but it seemed worth my time to tear out each green shoot. I did it thoroughly, scattering them in all directions, crushing the largest to pulp underfoot, rubbing the pulp into nothingness. By the time I was satisfied it was almost full dark. I heard a car motor start across the way and when I got again to a place where I could see the welfare house all was dark there. Receding red lights were almost out of sight up the river road. They turned north at the first crossroad, perhaps going to Shooken's meeting.

I hiked cautiously into the farm. There was still enough light so that I had no trouble making out a path.

When I was up on the front porch I beat heavily on the door, but no one came. After a time I tried the door. It opened to my touch. I went in carefully.

"Hey! Anyone home?" I yelled loudly. "I need to talk to someone."

No one came. No one answered.

I went up the steps and was immediately elated. On the third floor the doors were open to the rooms where Angler and the twins and Sam lived. I explored eagerly. Sam had his own room, the smallest room on the floor. I examined it in the darkness. There was a small window, up high. A little moonlight came through it. I found, in Sam's bureau, his few, pitiful things, ragged jeans, a couple of shirts. His room was as neat and clean as an operating room, the bed tautly made, hair brush and toilet articles arranged with geometric precision on the scarred, ancient bureau.

The bigger room was more cluttered. Inside it were four sets of bunk beds and one cot. There were multiple chests and bureaus along the walls. The drawers of several of the chests bulged with clothes, some of them expensive and with labels from a high-grade men's store I knew in Bington.

I pulled each occupied drawer out and checked the drawer and then above and behind it in the opening. I was soon rewarded with a variety of plastic packages. The larger ones were filled with brown, coarse weed. There were at least two varieties of powders in smaller packets. I presumed the weed was marijuana. I had no idea about the powders, maybe cocaine, angel dust, speed, or even heroin.

I found not much in the way of weapons except for a small, .22-caliber revolver Saturday-night special hidden in a glove in a drawer. I hefted it, thought about taking it, and then finally contented myself with breaking off the firing pin by jamming it into a floor crack and working it back and forth. I put it back in the drawer.

I checked under mattresses, in pillow cases, in nooks. I tapped walls and even examined the floorboards to see if any were loose, but could find nothing else.

I visited Kate's room. Here again the possessions were few, a few skirts, some jeans, and a top or two.

I found books stacked under her bed. The books weren't what I thought they'd be. They were love novels, nonpornographic, most of them in paperback with bright covers showing gorgeous girls and handsome men. Nurse and doctor books, historical romances. Sweet, little books. All of them seemed well thumbed.

I was back in the hall trying to decided what else to look over when, from far away, I thought I heard something approaching, a car motor.

I went quickly down the steps. By the time I was on the first floor I could see approaching lights.

I ran down the central hall and entered the kitchen. When the front door opened I went out the back door I'd already eased open and fled into the dark. There was enough light overhead to see. I moved quickly, but not so fast that I fell over anything, just moving along smartly.

I drove back to town.

On my office postage scale I weighed out what I'd taken. There was about nine ounces of pot, not really a lot, but substantial. There was a total of almost two ounces of powder, enough when poured out to cover my two hands cupped. It wasn't usable or available evidence. I'd secured it during an illegal search. They'd gotten my tires and my flower beds and finally me so that I'd notice them and so I had noticed them finally.

I flushed the powder down the office toilet. On my way home I stopped in a grocery and bought a can of lighter fluid. I dropped the plastic sacks of marijuana in the old barrel I had on the alley back of my apartment, a burning barrel. I sprayed the mess with lighter fluid and then sent it heavenward in thick, sweet smoke.

I shaved for the second time that day and took another long shower. After that was done I examined myself in the floor-length mirror that some past sybarite had installed on the back of my bathroom door. There I was, Honest Donald Robak, the female juvenile's friend. My right side was swollen a bit and still tender to the touch and there was a lesser bruise apparent on the left side, but the running had toughened me enough so that the bruises seemed superficial.

I examined myself all the way up to where my hair thinned and there gave it up as a bad job. I'd probably never be the type women fought over. If they ever did fight, then it seemed that the loser should win.

I dressed carefully in old, soft knit pants and my best Hickey Freeman jacket, a leftover from a time now five years in the past. That year I'd gotten a sudden, unexpected jury verdict and had celebrated. Afterward the jury verdict had vanished in the smoke of an appellate reversal.

I thought for a while about going down town to the Moose and having a few, then a huge steak, then taking a hack at Marla Rettner Tilden, partly because I was restless, partly to see what made Cherry and Marla tick.

I didn't go.

I decided that if she asked me again if her sister had done the dirty deed on the deceased Davidsons I'd have to say I thought so. I'm honest, if depraved. Even if Cherry hadn't been the primary mover, even if more people were involved, Cherry was deep enough in it to drown.

In a few weeks or a few months, we'd go to trial. Cherry could then take her starry-eyed chances on what the machinations of her boy friend Angler could accomplish.

I gave up worrying about it for a while and went to the Oasis, which is my favorite Bington place. They sell huge steaks there, cooked to perfection, and don't charge more than an even ton for them. If they water the Bourbon I can't tell after three or four.

Then, after the steak and the Bourbon, I did go past the Moose and got my idea of an after-dinner drink, which was one more E.T. and water. Marla was there.

I took my drink and got a table away from the action. In a bit Marla came and sat across from me.

"Hey now," she said in a low, conversational voice, "I keep getting these bad, anonymous calls about you. Some person who doesn't like you says you're a shyster, unclean, a cheat, and that you don't care about anyone except a man named Robak." She smiled to take the sting away.

"That's some of the good friends I've made during my employment representing your sister," I said.

"Stick with it," she said stoutly.

"I need to ask you something, Marla. On the night the Davidsons died someone made an anonymous call reporting it to the sheriff, bringing him to the scene. Do you know anything about that?"

She shook her head.

"I've been out around the place," I said. "There's the river plus the highway. I suppose on a still night a passer might have heard something. Do you remember what kind of night it was?"

"Yes. I remember because I got a call that night about Cheryl. It was calm enough, no rain, no wind."

"Thank you," I said. I wondered if she'd been the caller. It was possible, but not probable.

She smiled gently at me. "I get off in a little bit. Want to discuss things more at my place?"

I was tempted.

"I'd like to talk with you some more about Cheryl and her problems."

I wasn't sure I could stomach much more talk about Cheryl, at least for a while.

"Maybe another time," I said.

She wasn't used to rejection. I could read that in her eyes.

I was pretty certain that if we went to her place to talk about sweet Cherry then that's exactly what we would do. Age has made me less of a dreamer and more of a realist.

Coming home, I was very careful. I parked the LTD at Iron Mike's station and walked in, using back alleys, moving cautiously, but I saw nothing.

Inside my apartment, I remembered an old sleeping bag I'd bought in the past, back when my idea of a high time included an occasional night on the ground. I rummaged around and found it deep back in a closet. It still seemed in good shape and smelled faintly of moth balls.

The Coulson apartment and mine were joined by a communal back porch. I left the lights off in my kitchen and quietly went out my back door and used the key the Coulsons had left with me to enter their place. Inside I found the best place to lay out my sleeping bag was in their middle room, for them a sort of dining, television area. If anyone managed to track me this far and entered after me that someone would have to approach through a room and a half, either way, to take me.

I went back to my own place and sat thinking about it. I had no doubt that Angler and his friends would try again. I'd have to be punished. But with no one watching outside, with no one in waiting, I seemed safe for this night and could sleep in my own bed.

I turned on television and watched commercials selling various tapes and records interspersed with short breaks showing a war movie where people died in large numbers. Watching that, I fell asleep.

I slept well enough for a time.

Jo called around midnight. I turned off the television and answered.

"Hey there," I said into the phone, pleased, but groggy.

"Hey there yourself. Were you asleep?"

"Not really," I said, lying for love's sake. "Drowsing a tiny bit, maybe. I find I do that quite often at my advanced age."

"You sound like you've been asleep," she insisted. "Or maybe drinking too much." Jo didn't much like drinking, an old dislike that emanated from her first marriage.

"I haven't been drinking that much," I said a little stiffly. "Tell me about the vacation?"

"I went out to Malibu today. It was very pretty, fancy houses, surf and sand." She was silent for a moment. "I talked with a neighbor earlier this evening after trying to call you and not getting your phone to answer. She told me there was a story in the *Chronicle* and you were in another murder case."

"It's a juvenile matter," I said, deprecating it. "The girl's only sixteen years old."

"You told me you were going to avoid taking on things like that."

"I know, but business hasn't been that good. I needed the case. Besides, someone had to take it. The family hired me."

"I know about her family also." I could hear her sigh. Lawyers, she'd once told me, should write contracts and deeds, advise banks, settle estates, and wear dark, vested suits.

"For a while," she said slowly, "I was confused. I thought perhaps I'd stay out here. But I've decided to come home. I'll be there in a week. I'm tired of new places. I want to see Bington. If that offer's still open, I want to see you, Don."

"It's open. And I'm right here waiting for you," I said. *Outside it seemed to me that I heard something. A movement. A foot on a twig? The wind?*

She kissed me on the phone and I replied and we hung up.

I listened some more. Nothing. Not a sound out of the ordinary. But I'd lived through an old war and something within me remembered how I'd done it. Part of that time had been the product of luck, part knowledge, but a good part had been instinct.

I left the lights on and slipped quickly out my back door. From my back porch I surveyed a dark and silent yard. The moon was down. There was nothing to see, and yet there was *something*, very faint, a flickering of light, as if someone far away was drawing on an unshielded cigarette or trying to light my wall with a single firefly.

Something I'd heard, something I remembered, made me fear what I saw.

I went out the back door of the porch and loped quickly toward the alley. There I planned to stop again and see what was happening and from whence the flickering came.

The blast caught me at the alley's edge and blew me into a rolling ball. All the remembered thunders of my old war came back to me anew. I rolled, skinning myself a little, cinders and pebbles digging into my hands. Then I was in control again. I got up, a little dizzy.

The side of my apartment gushed smoke. There was a flicker of flame through the smoke. I ran that way, hoping there'd be no other blasts. The fire came from a window curtain. I jerked it out the gaping hole where once my window had been. I stamped the curtain into the ground, sending sparks flying. The inside of my apartment looked like a disaster area.

I stood and waited and watched. Lights came on all over the neighborhood. I saw some close neighbors peering out windows broken by the explosion. For a time I heard very little. It seemed to me that all sound came as if through deep water.

It wasn't long until police arrived. With them came Sheriff Abe Dorsett. By that time I could hear fairly well again.

The damage was substantial. There was a huge hole in the side of my middle room. Inside that room bits of blown debris had embedded themselves in ceiling and walls. Every bit of glass on my side of the house was broken. My bed was full of bits of wood and plaster and glass. Overhanging all was the pervasive smell of burned powder, sour and acrid.

"Dynamite," Sheriff Abe said. "Now I know what they wanted with the dynamite they stole."

I shook my head. "I'm probably an afterthought, Abe. If I were you I'd put a twenty-four-hour watch on the home of a Mr. Cecil Fitzgerald. He's a retired schoolteacher. The dynamite was stolen too long ago for it to have been intended, at least then, to be used against me."

"You think you know who set this off?" he asked.

"I think so." I told him who and why. I waited while he used his car radio to make calls.

"If they go to the Fitzgerald place we'll be there waiting for them."

I smiled. "You can't watch forever, Abe. Angler knows that. He's very patient. In the interim why don't you talk those people who run the welfare house out there into letting you search it. You might turn up something interesting in an exhaustive search. Don't bother too much with their rooms."

He gave me a look. "Why exclude their rooms?"

"A hunch, Abe. Only a hunch."

He kept watching me. "I got told when I got into this job that you ought to be watched. I think maybe I'll do that careful from now on."

I smiled. "It would be nice to be watched by someone involved in enforcement for a change."

I thought he was going to say something else, but then he shook his head.

I heard him use his radio once more. In another while a burly, well-dressed young man came into my yard. He introduced himself as a special agent for the Alcohol, Tobacco, and Firearms Agency. He asked a lot more questions.

Later, I got to use my sleeping bag in the Coulson apartment. I slept well again, but only for an indeterminate time.

CHAPTER XIII

A child, under some theories of law, can commit no crimes, except the crime of murder. All other actions of a child are mere infractions and should not be punished, but . . .

I came somewhat awake in their vehicle. I could move a little, but the movements weren't under my direction. I could feel my right arm lift and fall and I wondered dispiritedly what made it do that. I knew nothing of how they'd taken me.

They transported me in the back of a luxurious van, the twins up front, Angler in back with me. Now and then I'd force my eyes open. Above me, not very far and within easy reach, was the handle which opened the back door of the van. I willed myself to reach for it, but nothing came of it.

Angler watched happily from his plush seat.

"Keep tryin', old runner," he said fondly, perhaps reading my desire from my eyes. "It won't do you no damned good. No damned good at all." He smiled down at me, a smile of possession and promise. "We have a good time waiting for you. You've been invited out to a house warming. Guest of honor. Your police came and searched everywhere their small minds could think of, but not in exactly the right place. We watched them do it. Now they're gone."

At the welfare house they roughly carried me up dark steps, two flights of them. I was dumped on a hard floor and I heard the sound of a door being shut and then locked. I lay there.

"Move the van out behind the trees," I heard Angler order. "We've got to get cracking. Sooner or later that federal man will get tired of talking with the Allens and Sam and Kate and bring them back. We want to get everything done before they get back, no loose ends. You know time ain't helping us."

I fought with whatever it was that was keeping me unable to move. After a while a little co-ordination came back. I found I could will a few simple muscles to do a bidding and, after what seemed a very long time, those muscles would creak sturdily into action. It was like slow motion, but I kept working at it. In half an hour or so I managed to turn myself over so that I lay face-up. I got my right leg operating well enough so that I could push myself along and into a corner. It seemed to work far better than my left leg.

Now and then I could hear them moving, both in the hall outside and in other parts of the house. I could hear the sound of a hammer and what sounded to me like a wrecking bar. From what I'd overheard I assumed that the sheriff and the federal agent had come, searched the place, but not found Angler and/or the twins. So they'd apparently taken the Allens and Kate and Sam for further questioning.

I put my ear up against the wall and, among other sounds, I could hear their voices now and then.

I heard Angler say, "Come on. Move. They promised the Allens they'd bring everyone back in the early morning. And sooner or later they might get the idea of checking on us here again. So don't show any lights. Get the rest of the stuff worth saving into the van. Ball up the papers good. Shoot that charcoal stuff and those cans of gasoline on that old wood and let it soak in good. There's too much stolen stuff here for us to save much of it. We got to get a fire going good enough that no fire equipment will ever get it put out."

A smell came into the room. I thought I'd smelled something like it before at cookouts and picnics. My hands felt cold and lifeless and I was suddenly so afraid that I shook and my teeth began to rattle uncontrollably. Guest of honor at a house warming. I thought I knew what kind of house warming Angler meant.

I began to work harder, unwilling to just give up and die. Only one leg did well, the right one. I used it to push at the left, tug it up and push it down. With the help of my improving right leg I managed to raise myself up and sit against the wall.

It was very dark outside, moonless. I knew from my running that dawn came at this time of year between five and six in the morning so it had to be in advance of that time. My eyes were acclimated enough to the dark so that I could see the small, high window. I could also see the outline of bunk beds, a cot, and chests and bureaus: the big dormitory room. The window gave me a tiny surge of hope.

My right arm suddenly seemed much improved. I worked it as hard as I dared, swinging it feebly around, lifting it, letting it fall.

Using it and the good leg, I left the security of my position and agonizingly crawled to the window and lay below it, defeated again. The sill was beyond my reach. I pushed up hard with the good leg, once, twice. The second time I got my good hand over the sill and could use it to help pull myself up. Rising to stand was extremely hard, perhaps the most difficult thing I'd ever done in my life. Once up, my vision swam and I thought I was going to either faint or die. I leaned against the wall, braced and breathing hard, and finally did neither.

The window raised a little at my efforts with my good hand. It worked easily, but made a squeaking sound as it rose. As I listened I detected no change in the rhythms from outside, no loud voices, no sudden alarm.

In a while I had the window open halfway. I gulped in great breaths of night air. I stood on the one good leg and used my good arm to work the other arm up, down, up down.

Outside I heard someone come close to the door and begin to fumble with the lock. I jerked the window closed and let myself slide to the floor. I rolled a bit away from below the window.

I was saved by the darkness of the room and by the fact that my invader was slow in opening the lock.

He left the door open and came inside. Some light entered with him, some small light from the hall. I could see his eyes glisten.

"Hi there, Mr. Robak," he said happily. "I'm sorry it has to be so dark, but in a while we'll lighten it up for you."

"The police and some federal people are looking for you, Angler."

"Sure. We know about that. Maybe soon we'll let them find us. When it doesn't make any difference."

"What's all this about?"

He smiled at me. "You've been a bad problem, Mr. Robak. You've interfered in the plan. We used to sit around and talk about what would happen if the Davidsons ever got killed, me and the twins and Cherry. Then they did get killed, but you've made Cherry all unsure. You shouldn't have done that. What we were going to do for her would have worked."

"And because of that you set a bomb off at my apartment and now you're going to fire this house and burn me with it?" I asked.

"Sure. The bomb was originally for another friend, a very old friend. Mr. Fitz. But you got involved in our priorities." He nodded down at me. "How'd you know it was there? We saw you come busting out of the house. Too bad, too bad. How'd you know?" His voice was mildly curious.

I waited. He really didn't care how I'd known.

"I told you about those depositions and yet you got us served for them. You stuck your nose in the bishop's doings. You smelled around old Fitz. Suddenly the welfare's gotten interested out here, the food, the place itself. You fooled around in our stuff. You should have done like I said. It would all have been all right then."

"You're not right in the head, Angler."

His face colored enough for me to see the change even in the dim light. "Not me. No. You and your world are wrong. You got all those complex and insane laws. You say we kids are property and you lock us away and forget us when we don't do like you tell us. You say we've got to go to stupid schools, that we can't smoke or drink even when you do, that we've got to be in at certain times. You tell us no drugs, no grass, ever. You won't let us drive although our reactions are better than yours. You've got the money and the power even when some of us are lots smarter than you are." He shook his head in mock wonderment. "Why should it be that way? I'm smarter than you are. I know all you know and a lot more. I can read one of your books that takes you days in only minutes. I know almost all. I should be the one to control my world. The drugs and the stuff we've stolen gave us enough money. So I've decided to run things. I've figured out a good way. Bishop Shooken is going to take me into his ministry. Would you believe, Rev. Angler? I can talk and lie as good as him. I'll have my own flock soon, young ones, mean ones." He smiled down at me again. "Shooken respects me. I showed him some photos I took of him and Cherry when she was out. I keep them in the van." He nodded to himself. "She was all he came around for at the end. He was worn out on those Davidsons. They drank too much and didn't pay their share." He reached in his pocket and brought out a gadget of tape and springs and clothespins. "Know what this is?"

I nodded. It was a match gun.

"Put a lucifer match in it and when the pin hits the head of the match it shoots it out and lights it. Even in a car moving at thirty miles an hour I can put a match in a wastebasket on the other side of the street three times out of four." He nodded. "Doesn't look like much of a death weapon, but it is one." He smiled fondly down at me. "In a little while I'm going to make you a part of my newest plan, Mr. Robak. And the three of us have decided that from now on we're going to dispose of any adults who get in our way like you did, judges, prosecutors, sheriffs, anyone at all. That's what the bishop preaches. But we'll be smart. We won't leave any evidence and we won't give any statements. If we're charged we're going to file motions for speedy trial, we're going to conduct our own defense. And we'll win." He nodded down at me. "We want you to stay warm thinking on that."

"Did you kill the Davidsons?" I asked.

He gave me a look of surprise. "Far as I know, Mr. Robak, Cherry killed them. Sure she did. She was the only one who could have done it. Way I figured it out was she came to when that old man was messing with her and his wife helping. The good old Bishop Shooken wanted her too, but Cherry was picky. We'd tell him when she had bad spells and he'd come around then. To help that along that night I gave her some stuff. Angel dust. Really set her off. But she got so bad that night Bishop Shooken didn't want to fool with her, screaming and scrambling around, hitting out. So he took off and the Davidsons came up. We went into our room and stayed there, just like the statements said." He nodded spitefully. "And maybe you think you got all our stuff when you raided out here, but you missed the most of it. Plenty left. We'll move it and hide it. But stealing our stuff did make you our number one hate man."

"I could get Cherry off for you yet," I said. "I could create enough smoke to do that. You don't know how it works. You'd just have to go along a little. If you only wait a little longer it will be your world, Angler. As smart as you are, as much as you know, it would all come to you soon. Kill me and you're an outlaw."

He smiled. "We're going to do our very best to make sure we don't get blamed. And no matter what they'd do to me I can get out. I can get Cherry out of wherever they put her. I can escape from anywhere. Believe me that I can, Mr. Robak. I've read all the books, I know all the locks. I'd get away and then just go to one of a dozen places and vanish. London, Paris, Mexico." He gave me an intense look. "Tell me why you had to steal our stuff and tear up our pot field?"

"Because you came after me. Because you ice-picked my car tires and tore up my flowers."

"We stopped you to reason with you, but I didn't know about the other stuff, your tires and flowers. I didn't tell them to do that. They shouldn't have done it." He smiled once more. "But I guess we'll get the last lick in, huh, Mr. Robak?"

I looked into the insanity of his eyes. I saw no mercy there, no reprieve.

"Bishop Shooken tells his fools that there's soon to be a retribution day for lawyers like you," Angler said softly. He looked down at me, inspecting me closely. "I see you've managed to move a little from where we dropped you, but I doubt you'll get far. That's an animal tranquilizer we shot you with. I mix it with some other stuff and it does funny things. It sure works good. I used it on a kid we run onto down by the river who gave us some lip. They'll never find him. You don't have long to wait now, Mr. Robak."

He moved to the door and closed it with a final thump. I heard the lock click shut again.

"So long, Mr. *Donald* Robak," I heard one of the twins call to me from the hall outside.

I got back up to the window and opened it again. I took my good arm and worked it up and down some more. I forced the bad one to move. I found I could totter precariously along the wall. The bad arm was even a little better, not close to normal, but better. I could tell the hand at the end of it to make a fist and it would do so eventually. Once made, the fist seemed strong enough.

I searched about the room slowly, seeking a weapon. Given time I might have taken one of the bunk beds apart and perhaps fashioned a club out of part of a side rail, but there were rusted screws and they defeated me. I found one thing. On the floor, kicked under a bunk bed, was a match gun. On a bureau I found three matches. One of them was moist and when I touched it the striking head fell away. The other two seemed all right. There was no way to test them. I put match gun and matches in my shirt pocket.

I doubted that they'd even thought about the fact that I might make it out a window. They were big, bulky boys, fully grown. The window probably seemed too small for exit to them. But diet and the running the past few years had reduced my weight to the same figure I'd carried as a high school senior. I thought I could get through the window. The question was whether I could lower myself down to what lay below without falling, and then get in another window to the second floor. I remembered there was a porch. That should help.

I pushed on one of the bunk beds, but it and its companions were either nailed or bolted to the floor. The bureau wasn't. It was bulky and made faint, squeaking sounds which frightened me, but it moved across the floor. I got it near the window and removed the top drawers. There was a post down the center. It was thin and didn't seem substantial, but it would have to stand up.

I tied shirts to jeans. I added my own shirt, first taking the match gun and matches from it and putting them into my pants pocket. I knotted the mess together, then tied one end around the center post.

Using the bureau for help, I made it up to the window. I climbed the lower drawers after pulling them out like stair steps. I threw the clothes rope out against the side of the house. I then got good arm and good leg entwined in the rope and slipped and slid perilously down to the narrow porch roof, which I found twenty feet or so below. I found an open window there and entered as stealthily as possible, thumping around some, particularly when the bad leg caved in as I crawled through.

I stood inside for a moment, breathing deeply. The world grew dim around me and I was glad the condition had waited for this time instead of occurring as I was coming down the rope.

I was in the bedroom of the keepers of the house, the Allens. An old, canopied bed stood in the center of the room. A sign on the wall nearest the bed read, "God Bless Our Home and Children." There was a door beyond the bed. I moved that way and slid it open. Above me, on the third floor, I could hear them.

"All set?" Angler asked impatiently. "Check on Robak once more, Joe. He'd moved some last time I looked."

That didn't sound good. I moved out the door, still unable to walk quickly.

I heard the sound of a lock being worked. I kept moving toward the stairs.

"Jesus, he ain't here," Joe called loudly. "He's got out the window somehow."

I snatched the match gun out and loaded it, fingers trembling. In a moment, if they looked down, they'd have to see me.

"Stay where you are up there," I called. "First move down and I'll fire the place." I remembered something Martha Angler had said. "Stay where you are, Junior."

It didn't stop them. Someone dim up there fired down at me from the deeper darkness at the top of the stairs. The shot came from a heavy caliber weapon, certainly not the .22 I'd tampered with. The bullet buzzed nearby. I thought the gunman was Angler. I fired my lonely match up into the hallway above. It streaked up into the darkness and died.

"Get him," Angler screamed angrily. "Get him!"

I saw and heard the flash of another shot and with it there came a vast explosion of heat. It was as if someone had dumped gasoline on a bonfire. A shock wave buffeted me, forced my weak legs into total collapse, and sent me rolling toward and then down the steps. One boy came falling after me, thumping down, his shirt and trousers smoldering. At the bottom of the steps the sparks in his shirt burst into torches and he rolled and writhed on the floor. It was one of the twins. He screamed something incomprehensible at me.

I pulled a heavy curtain from a window and rolled him in that, snuffing the worst of the flame, but he must have gotten some charcoal-lighter fluid or gasoline on him because here and there, where the curtain didn't cover, he continued to burn.

The fire moved downward toward us. I pulled the boy with me toward the front door, sliding him, pushing and rolling. He muttered and screamed now and then. Eventually I had him in the open yard. I rolled him over and over until all flames stopped.

Somehow Angler had made it out onto the roof. Perhaps there were stairs up that I'd not found in my checking the house. I could see him up there, moving, cat-quick, forty or fifty feet high. He yelled something into the night and slapped at his hair. Whatever he called was lost in the vast, soaring sound of the roaring fire.

"Jump," I yelled. "Jump!"

There was one tree in the yard near the house. Its leaves close to the fire crackled and shriveled. Angler moved up the roof and in the direction of that tree, perhaps thinking to jump into it. But as he moved I saw the roof collapse downward. For a moment he teetered on the edge of the collapsed area and then he vanished into the brightness.

Far away I could hear the sound of approaching sirens.

I examined the twin. He was breathing shallowly. Once he called out something in a low voice and I thought it might have been "Joe." I wasn't sure. Maybe it was "Jack." His shirt was charred away in spots and hair and eyebrows were pretty much gone. There was a huge bump on the left side of his head where he'd hit something on his way down the stairs. One eye was part open, but it didn't see me.

He was still breathing when the firemen came.

CHAPTER XIV

The purpose of the juvenile code is not to exact punishment on delinquent children, but to educate them, train them, and make them ready to be good citizens of this . . .

It was several days before I could get to juvenile detention in the jail. During that passage of time several things of importance occurred.

I took Marla into the jail with me.

Cherry sat quietly on her bunk. A tiny transistor radio beside her played pop music. It wasn't very loud, but it wasn't a very big radio either. It seemed to doing the best it could.

"They're going to let you out very soon, Cherry," I said.

"They're going to place you in another house, but I'm going to try again to get you," Marla said to her. "Mr. Robak said he'd help, if I wanted."

She gave us both a listless look.

"Angler's dead. They say Angler's dead."

"He's dead," I admitted.

"I should have run you off the very first thing," she said in a low voice. "It all had to be your way and now Angler's dead." She cursed me for a moment or so in the same low voice, quite good, using expressions she hadn't heard in jail.

When she slowed, I said, "He was trying to burn the house down with me in it, Cherry. One of them took a shot at me and that set off the fire." I wasn't absolutely sure of that, but I wasn't going to change it. I thought the match I'd shot upward had died.

Beside me Marla moved restlessly. "The prosecutor now thinks it could just as well have been them as you after what they tried to do to Mr. Robak. They had keys to the doors and could get in and out from them somehow even when they were locked from outside. They set off dynamite at his house, too. But you're going to get out because there isn't any case left."

Cherry was still watching me. "I wish they'd have blown you up," she said. "I wish that bad." She got up from the bunk and walked slowly, like an old woman, toward the bars. I saw her eyes were red from crying. When she got close to the bars she brought the sharp-clawed fingers of her right hand out through the bars at my eyes, very intent about it, but I moved back quickly and she missed.

"Maybe they'll give me my knife back. If they don't I'll get another and come for you, you son-of-a-bitch bastard," she promised.

"You'll change your mind later," I said heartily. "After you've had a chance to think about it."

She shook her head, still intent.

I moved as close as I dared. "I'm sure you knew Angler was after me and you didn't do a thing about it. That doesn't make me happy with you, either. And if you'd like, I can get you that hypnotist any time you're ready for one, assuming you now think you're not guilty of anything and I'm guilty of murdering your boy friend."

Her eyes fell.

Marla said, "Go on for now, Mr. Robak. Let me talk with her. It'll be all right."

"Sure," I said, glad to go. I walked on out, taking the adult-area route. The man who'd been doing the cursing during my first trip in to see Cherry lay on his bunk. He gave me the finger when I went past.

I stopped, perplexed.

"Told them to put me in Sunday solitary, didn't you, Robak? I'll see you around when I get out. You better wait and watch behind you. I'm going to have a great big piece of you."

I thought about protesting my innocence, but didn't think it would do any good.

I smiled at him instead. "You better come from behind, rummy, or you'll never get that job done on your best day." I kept walking.

He cursed me a little, but not nearly as inventive about it as Cherry.

They'd moved Kate to the other juvenile home. It was a little more pleasant than the one that had burned, but it could have been constructed by the same carpenters, designed by the same architects, and mutilated by the same passage of years. The house was American ramshackle; the yard was worn into mud and weeds.

I parked the LTD in front. I was now keeping it with me again, not leaving it with Iron Mike. I needed it as I was staying temporarily in a motel. My landlord had been pretty sour about the huge hole in his wall, plus all the interior damage. The last time I'd talked with him he'd been having trouble with his insurance carrier. I hated to think about moving. I was used to the apartment and Jo liked it all right. Maybe the bank would make me a loan and I could buy the place.

The man who answered the door when I rang a tinny-sounding bell had a black beard, was thirtyish, and wore paint-stained pants plus a dirty T-shirt with a design on it from *Star Wars*. I'd seen him before someplace. I thought maybe he'd been one of the men in black suits with Bishop Shooken.

"What you need, bub?"

"I'd like to see one of your boarders. Miss Kate James. My name is Robak and I'm a lawyer."

"I know you," he said sourly. "Kate!" he bawled.

I stepped in the open door. In a few moments Kate came hesitantly down the steps. When she saw me her face cleared and she came swiftly on.

"They're bringing Cherry here today," she bubbled. "Mr. Koontz told me." She nodded at the beard, who stood in the hall morosely watching us.

"Yes, I'd heard that," I said. "She's sort of angry at me right now."

"She'll soon get over it." She looked around and saw Koontz still watching us. She took my arm and led me back out the door. "Come on."

"Lunch soon. Better be ready if you want food," he called after her spitefully.

"Him and his wife aren't bad people," she confided on the porch. "Just nosy."

"Better than the Davidsons and the Allens?"

She nodded. "Better than Davidsons, anyway. I never

really got to know the Allens. You okay? I read some about it in the paper."

"I'm all right. A little sore. Nothing much."

"Was there anything special you wanted?" she asked politely.

I looked around. The porch was empty and Kate had closed the front door behind us.

"I'd like for you to keep Cherry away from me until she gets over her mad. I don't want to wake up some night and find Cherry, knife in hand, in my apartment. I don't want to come out of court and find her waiting for me around some dark corner."

She smiled. "I'll sure do my best."

"Please, Kate. The way I have it figured, you owe me that."

"How's that, Mr. Robak? How do I owe you?"

"You got away with it. It worked. Now everything is over and okay."

"If you mean that Angler got what he should have gotten then I agree with you. He used to do mean things to Sam and me, but he stopped after he found a snake under his bed and had some other trouble. I'm sorry about Joe, but only a little. He was an oaf. They tell around that his brother's not right in the head in addition to being burned awful bad."

"He hasn't made much sense," I said.

She waited, eyes cool.

"You got what you wanted," I repeated. "I think those Davidsons came bothering after you for fun, so you knifed them. If things were normal they were stoned and it was easy. No one did any blood-alcohol tests on them, but I'll bet they were stoned to the eyeballs."

"They did bother me once," she admitted tranquilly. "It was scary. Sam helped scare them off me that time." She watched me from some distant, unassailable place. "Sam's back in the kitchen. Maybe you'd want to talk with him, too?"

"But you figured that sometime they weren't going to get scared off so you planned it and killed them, Kate," I said, ignoring the patter about Sam.

"No. I never did that." She gave me a smile and brushed a hand through her hair. "Remember, I was locked in my room."

"You were locked in when the sheriff came. It didn't mean a single thing. The door had to be open for Cherry to get out, so we start with that. I figure the Davidsons' key turned the locks, but left your door open. That's the only way for Cherry to have gotten out. You said she locked you in behind her, but you're the only witness to that. I think you did what you wanted to do, then locked yourself conveniently in. When you were out Cherry was in the midst of something, probably an epileptic fit complicated by drugs given her by Angler. I think you knew about that also. And you'd seen Cherry have her attacks before. You'd studied her carefully, become an expert on her. You took off your clothes so you wouldn't get any blood on them. There was even time for a shower before you called the sheriff and closed the door behind you."

She shook her head. "It's all over now," she said confidently. "You're just making this up to have some fun with me—is that it, Mr. Robak?"

"No. I'm here for a purpose, Kate. I know you did it. Too many things told me. I had Dr. Buckner check Cherry over. He said that her killing the Davidsons and not remembering it was a medical improbability; that I'd never get anyone to testify to it. The thing that confused me for a while was that Cherry was willing to believe she did the job. I think she was unconscious, but she knew Angler could get out of his cage one way or the other. She thought Angler had done it or had it done for her. That's why she didn't want anything to do with my offer of a hypnotist. She didn't want to know what had happened. One way or another it would be bad news for her. She was convinced he could get her out of it, so she just went along." I shook my head, remembering Angler standing above me in the dorm room while I waited for my housewarming. "When Angler thought I was about to go up in smoke, when he had no reason to lie, he told me he'd not done it and thought Cherry had. So you did a good little bit of hand magic. You convinced them both. After all, who'd believe that little old you did the murders? I think you probably planted the knife with Cyclops when you knew Cherry wanted one. I'll bet if I took that knife and carried it to the shops in and around Bington I might find the place you bought it, even get someone to identify you."

She shook her head confidently. "No, you couldn't do that, Mr. Robak."

"I don't want you to confess, Kate. I'm just theorizing a little. My job in this one is done. Cherry's out from under. The police are convinced that Angler and his pals did the whole thing. I helped clench that for them when I described seeing Angler up on that burning roof and said I'd seen him with a key in his possession to the dorm room. If he could get up on the roof then, they now believe he could have gotten out of his room to kill the

Davidsons. That's the accepted theory. Even the prosecutor, who hated doing it, bought it when he figured out I had a good chance of getting a jury to go along. He didn't want egg on his face right around election time." I smiled down at her as she watched me intently. "I wound up a hero in the press. He decided he'd be a loser in a trial. I had him and he knew it. So it's done for sweet Cherry. She'll get out, but she'll get out carrying a big hate for me. Angler taught her that transgressors have to be punished. I'm her main man now. I don't want to have to hurt her. I didn't want to hurt anyone. All I ever wanted to do was my job, my way."

"Your problem and hers."

"Yours too, Kate. You're a very smart girl. If Cherry ever gets close to me and I get the chance, I'm going to lay the same word on her that I'm now laying on you. What I'm hoping is that you're smart enough to watch close until someone else gets her attention, some new boy. After that she'll maybe forget me. It shouldn't take forever. Like you said, boys like her."

"There's a very handsome one here," she said carefully. "Not here in the house just now because he stole a car last night. Tall boy with great, blondish hair. I thought of him and Cherry together the first time I saw him."

"I think you called the sheriff that night, Kate. Right after you did it and showered up. Maybe you even wore Cherry's clothes."

"Remember when she wanted to fire you and I helped talk her out of it?" she asked sincerely.

"I remember. I figured it was maybe better the devil you knew than a new one. Whoever took over for me would contact me, know all I knew, so you'd gain nothing with another lawyer. Besides, I liked you."

"I like you too, Mr. Robak." She smiled a gentle smile. "I'd sure want you to represent me if I ever got in trouble. Of course I hope I won't."

"Someone told me that friendship was too complicated for you for a long time, Kate. Is it still?"

She shook her head.

"Did they hurt you, Kate?"

Her eyes went opaque. "No. Not really. I don't know what you mean, Mr. Robak. Once they hurt Sam. Beat him badly."

"You have to understand, Kate, that life isn't like those pure-love books you read and hide away. I think you need to talk to a psychiatrist soon."

"I have talked to psychiatrists. They tell me I'm fine." She looked up at me, fifteen years old, looking younger than that. "I don't think you believe one bit of these crazy things you're saying." She smiled at me, a good, brave smile. She knew and I knew that there wasn't a bit of hard evidence against her. Even if I found she'd bought the knife Cyclops had supplied Cherry it meant little or nothing.

"You can bet I'll do the best I can for you with Cherry. She ought to thank you for what you've done, not be mad at you. I'm going to tell her that a dozen times a day."

"Get her out where the boys can see her, Kate," I directed. "Keep her away from me and mine. I think I'm about to get married."

She gave me a look of wonder, as if trying to figure out what someone of my advanced years would be accomplishing with marriage.

"That's nice, Mr. Robak. That's real nice."

"You stay away from me, too, Kate."

Her eyes flickered. "Don't joke with me." She cocked her head and looked up at me. "Did you hear about Bishop Shooken and the pictures?"

"No," I said, but I had heard that all wasn't well for the good bishop.

"Someone must have found some pictures of him with a young girl. Her face had been carefully cut out of all the pictures. She and the bishop were doing bad things. I heard lots of the bishop's congregation got pictures like that in the mail." She smiled, real malice in her eyes.

I nodded. Nothing had yet appeared in the Bington *Chronicle*, but I'd passed Gates Taine on the street that morning and he'd winked broadly at me and made a circle with thumb and forefinger.

"Good-bye, Kate."

"You take care, Mr. Robak."

"I do the best I can."

I left her on the porch and went out to the LTD. As I drove away I saw her wave to me once.